QHE!

THE PROPHETS OF EVIL

A mysterious quasi-religious movement calling itself The Prophets of the Prophet was causing grave nation-wide concern. Secret agents successfully infiltrated into the central group emerged as demented idiots powerless to reveal the truth. Only one man was capable of penetrating the barriers—and that man was Qhe, warrior of light and ruler of the remote Pashman. With Willard, his brother in faith, he embarked on a mission that was to bring them face to face with evil in its most demonic form. Evil that threatened even Qhe's magic and prayers as he struggled for the survival of the planet Earth . . .

QHE!
THE PROPHETS OF EVIL

W.·.W.·.

A STAR BOOK
published by
W. H. ALLEN

A Star Book
Published in 1976
by W. H. Allen & Co. Ltd.
A Howard & Wyndham Company
44, Hill Street, London W1X 8LB

Printed in Great Britain by
Richard Clay (The Chaucer Press), Ltd., Bungay, Suffolk

ISBN 0 352 39852 3

THE PROPHETS OF EVIL

ONE

The making of diamonds does not belong to the lore of magic and witchcraft and, yet, it is a truly miraculous process. We have all learnt at school how, over thousands of years, simple black coal can be compressed and compressed until it forms those sparkling white and yellow gems for which men are so greedy.

We learn also how a caterpillar, a furry little slug, can turn itself into one of nature's most beautiful creatures, a butterfly. And then there are all the other everyday miracles: tadpoles turn into frogs; small eggs hatch golden eagles; seeds burst into flowers. All this we know! But what of men? What of you and me?

What miracles can occur in the cycle of a member of the human race? The secret magical doctrines have always promised that man can become superman – that you or I can become like a godling. But these doctrines also promise that the path to this supreme goal is the most tortuous passage that any being can attempt to travel. It is as if, like coal, a man's personality must be squeezed and moulded until it too becomes as like a diamond.

Finely cut glass can look, even to the eye of an expert, like a perfect diamond, but smash it with a steel hammer ... Similarly, throughout the ages, some men have pretended to be supermen. Of the frauds some have been genuinely deluded, but others have been adepts of evil, working towards their own malicious and selfish ends. But how can an ordinary person tell the difference between the true saint and the absolute imposter? Normally, time is the judge – the passage of the years sifts out the good from the evil. But if there is no time, what then? There must be a battle ... A war for truth.

... In the huge wood-panelled hall of the chateau near

Grenoble in southern France the group of one hundred and fifty men and women were silent. Their faces were grave and sombre, yet their eyes shone with an excited and nervous expectancy. More than half were Arabs and they were immaculately dressed in the most expensive hand-tailored suits from Savile Row and Saint Honore. They had all been waiting now for just over an hour, but if needed they would have waited longer – infinitely longer.

They hardly dared to look at each other – the promise of what was about to take place thrilled them to their very core.

'And now your oath of secrecy!' The voice echoed around the hall, apparently coming from nowhere. 'Any man or woman who wishes to leave may do so now.'

No one moved. There was a pause for a minute and then everyone without exception and in unison produced a small razor blade. Holding the blades in their right hands, they dug the sharp edges into the palms of their left hands, creating thin deep cuts in their skin.

'Do you pledge your secrecy?' the voice echoed again.

Without hesitation, the people raised their left hands in the air, allowing a small trickle of blood to run down their wrists.

'We do!' they affirmed together.

'So be it!'

The double doors at the end of the hall swung open and the small crowd fell immediately to their knees and looked down at the floor. Three men now entered the chamber, a European dressed in flowing purple robes, a Persian dressed in robes of black, and a Japanese in deepest scarlet. They were slim men with long flowing hair and wore gentle expressions on their clean shaven faces. Side by side they made their way slowly to the opposite end of the hall where they mounted a small platform.

'Look up now,' the European said calmly.

'See us,' said the Persian.

'Watch and know,' intoned the Japanese.

The men and women raised their heads, but hardly dared look at the three men who stood so majestically above them.

'Seekers of knowledge,' the Japanese addressed them, 'we bring you truth. You have asked; we shall answer. Miracles and light we bring you as we herald the dawn of a new age, as we herald the coming of the new . . .'

But he did not finish the sentence, only allowing a mysterious smile to cross his lips.

'To receive you must give,' the Persian told them.

'And we shall give you the greatest gift of all – the light of the Lord.'

'The Lord!' the three of them said together, vibrating their voices so that the whole hall trembled.

'The Lord,' they repeated. 'The Lord, the light. He came before with a sword of fire and so he comes again. Nothing now will stop him. Nothing, nothing!'

'Here, child, come here.' The European pointed down at a young Egyptian.

As if in a trance the man approached the platform and stood, looking dazed and bewildered, up into the eyes of the man who had called him.

'Closer,' he was ordered.

The European laid his hands on the Egyptian's head and the people who watched thought that they could see the power flowing into their comrade. The young man's eyes opened as far as they could and then rolled back.

'Allah!' he cried, apparently in ecstasy. 'Allah! The hand of God is upon me.'

His head dropped back and as his face filled with bliss, he crumpled unconscious to the floor.

'By the power of he who comes do we do this,' the Japanese told them and pointed his outstretched hand at the crowd who drew back, blinking.

'Who else desires bliss?' the Persian asked.

'I, I, I,' the people there shouted.

'And who will be next?'

'I, I, I,' they shouted again.

Whimpering and with tears in her eyes, a woman pushed her way forward.

'Ask and you shall receive,' she was told as hands were

laid upon her head.

She screamed in joyful anguish and then she, too, collapsed to the floor. The other people were now in a frenzy of religious excitement. Every man and woman there wanted this extreme blessing and began to push towards the three men in robes. These three, however, just looked calmly, almost uncaringly, back at them. The anguished people reaching for them even more.

In unison, the three then raised their hands and the crowd was silent and still.

'Do you believe?' they were asked.

'We believe,' they screamed back.

'Do you believe?' they were asked again.

'Yes, yes!' they shouted.

The device was repeated and the tension and atmosphere increased second by second. Just at the moment when it seemed that their frenzy could not be taken any higher, the Persian in his black robes dropped crosslegged on the platform. He folded his arms across his chest and raised them up to the heavens. Imperceptibly at first, but then totally obviously, his body rose a few inches into the air.

Instantaneously the people fell deathly silent. The Persian's hands seemed to stretch higher into the air and his body now rose further, definitely floating two feet above the platform.

'Allah! Allah!' some of the Arabs moaned.

But one of the men watching, a Frenchman, could not succumb. For him, this was trickery, some form of evil mass hypnosis. He was sick to the core of seeing these people duped, and found the atmosphere unbearable, claustrophobic. He knew that he had to remain silent and not be discovered, but there was something about this whole scene that made his very soul shudder with disgust. With immense effort, he restrained and calmed himself. His eyes were fixed on the man in his black robes who was now floating as much as five feet in the air. The Frenchman shook his head. No, he told himself, he was in no trance: what he was seeing was real. There had to be wires or some theatrical conjurer's contraption. His mind became obsessed with discovering the invisible cords that held the Persian in the air and irresistibly he found himself walking towards the platform to discover and study them. Finally, standing only a few feet away, he screwed up his eyes and focused every ounce of concentration on the space around the Persian's body. But he could see nothing except a thin halo of glimmering silver light. He shook his head. No, his mind screamed, this is not possible! Not possible! Not possible!

The Persian smiled down at him and nodded. The Frenchman looked back up into the sorcerer's eyes and immediately looked away, falling whimpering to his knees. A few seconds later, he was carefully lifted by three white-suited attendants and carried out of the hall.

* * * * *

Two hundred yards away from the main gate to the chateau, two senior French internal security officers waited in their large black Citroen saloon. They were relaxed, chain-smoking Gauloises.

'Stupid business,' one of them said.

'Complicated,' the other replied and sighed. 'But if anyone can get in there, it's Henri.'

'Sure,' the first snorted. 'Henri and some religious fanatics. He'll find it easier than dealing with the Gestapo during the war!'

Both men laughed and then fell silent with confident smiles across their mouths. They had worked together in the Resistance, then in Algeria and recently had helped break the French heroin connection. Henri, their senior officer and their toughest operative in the agency, could surely deal with this one blindfold.

They picked up their binoculars as the gates to the chateau opened and within seconds had triggered the ignition on their car and screeched down the road to pick up their tottering comrade. His eyes were unable to focus on anything and he was burbling like a demented child.

TWO

Holding the enormous diamond, the size of a pigeon's egg, between his thumb and forefinger, Qhe smiled mischievously at the two journalists from Paris Match. They stood by an open window on the twenty-first floor of the International Gems office block and they had a superb view of Marseilles, her harbour and the glittering blue Mediterranean beyond.

'This little gem is virtually priceless,' Qhe told them. 'For centuries it was in the Vatican. Would you like to see?'

Both journalists, the man with his notebook and the young woman with her cameras, nodded slightly impatiently. They had been with His Majesty now for almost two hours and still had not been able to talk seriously with him.

'You're certain you want to see it?' he asked again and, once more, they nodded.

His smile broadened.

'Well then – catch!'

Without warning, he flicked the diamond towards them and the open window. Instantaneously they panicked, trying desperately to prevent the loss of the million pound stone. The man's arms flailed as it struck his wrist and recoiled towards the corner of the window. The woman dove to her right and grabbed frantically for it. She seemed to grasp it, but then lost it and then grasped it again. She clutched it to her chest and her suntanned face grimaced, caught between the relief of saving the diamond and the disaster of dropping her very expensive cameras. She hardly dared look down to see what had happened to them.

'They're quite safe,' Qhe told her, for at the moment that he had flicked the stone he had darted forward to save her equipment.

'Monsieur, Your Majesty,' the male journalist protested,

'you could have lost if for ever – irretrievably – a disaster! That was no joke.'

The girl was now blushing furiously, certain that in some way His Majesty had set this up to make a fool of her. What made it worse for her was the presence of the two other strangers in the room: explorer James Carrington and the anonymous man in the pinstripe suit who appeared to be His Majesty's private secretary.

'It cannot be a real diamond,' she said defensively.

'But it is,' Qhe answered, 'a real gem . . . just like you.'

Her blush deepened.

'You are one of the most agile people that I have ever met,' he continued. 'It is a pleasure to know you. I was merely demonstrating my immediate trust and affection for you.'

'Bravo,' the explorer Carrington enthused. 'His Majesty accepts few people so readily.'

The girl's expression now turned to one of acute embarrassment. What had been said seemed to be sincere and, for some strange reason, it gave her a deep sense of pleasure.

'Give him back his diamond,' her colleague said impatiently. 'It's obvious that this visit has been incorrectly timed and that His Majesty has not actually planned to speak to us.' He now turned to Qhe and bowed. 'We apologize for disturbing you.'

Qhe looked back at the journalist and frowned.

'And I too apologize,' he said. 'I had no idea you had so little time. We shall, therefore, get down to it immediately. Please follow me.'

He led the whole party from the room and down a long corridor. As they walked, he asked James Carrington whether he minded the journalists being there.

'If you think it's safe,' Carrington replied.

'I'm certain it will interest them. What you are about to see, or experience,' he informed the two journalists, 'will, I hope, help you in your researches. You are the first people from the press with whom I have done this. I have an intuition that I should help you with your article on the occult and mysticism. I don't know why . . .'

'And what exactly are we about to see?'

'Magic,' Qhe answered simply.

'Can I photograph it?' the girl asked.

'You *may*,' Qhe answered, 'but whether you *can* is another matter.'

They now entered a lift which took them up another floor in the building. The moment that the doors slid open, they were in a completely new atmosphere. The lighting was subdued, the walls were covered in violet and saffron silk, and there was the gentle scent of myrhh incense floating in the air. They passed into a circular room paved in white marble and in which stood the charcoal burner and the incense. Qhe clapped his hands and immediately two young boy servants from his home country of Pashman appeared. They were dressed in white robes and, like their king, their light coffee-coloured faces were finely featured and aristocratically handsome. One of them carried a large bronze jug and the other held a bowl and towel.

'If you would all wash your hands,' Qhe requested. 'A slight cleansing is needed.'

All of them now washed their hands and faces while the girl moved hurriedly around the room shooting pictures of the scene, stopping only for a minute to wash her own hands and face. Qhe clapped his hands again and the two boys left the room to be replaced by a third who carried a small charcoal burning incense holder on the end of three lengths of chain. Qhe nodded, clasped his hands together across his chest and bowed as the thurible was swung nine times in his direction. He then took the thurible himself and asked the two journalists to stand side by side and bow to him. Instinctively the girl raised her camera to photograph him . . . and Qhe laughed.

'Please,' he begged. 'You won't be safe otherwise.'

He laughed again, this time at the look of incredulity on the man's face.

'I know very well that you have covered many dangerous scenes,' Qhe told him, 'but, if for nothing else, just do it to humour me.'

The Frenchman shrugged and then bowed.

'Thank you. Now, as I swing the incense towards you, imagine that the smoke is filled with particles of shimmering light which purify the aura around you, which purify your electric bodies. Just use your imaginations.'

He swung the thurible towards them and they both started, feeling a slight electric shock.

'Very satisfactory.'

He then sensed Carrington and the other quiet man in his immaculate pinstripes.

'Are we ready, Willard?'

'Wouldn't say no,' Willard answered. 'Quite nice to do a bit of work like this for a change.'

'May I ask who this gentleman is?' the French journalist asked.

'Willard,' Qhe answered. 'One of the greatest wizards this side of the Himalayas – he and I have known each other for years . . . thousands of years.'

'Thousands and thousands,' Willard added. 'If the three of you would care to go in, His Majesty and I will join you in a minute.'

He opened a door and the two journalists and James Carrington entered a second room. Carrington had been in it once before, but the other two looked round in amazement. The floor was laid in exquisite mosaics forming patterns of crosses, pentacles and magical signs which were unknown to them. It had five walls, on each of which was an inlaid gold cross, and the ceiling was a stained glass dome which shone brilliantly in the sunlight. Against one of the walls was an altar in the shape of a perfect cube on which stood two golden candlesticks, a cut glass crystal vase with one white rose in it, a golden goblet and a wand. Above this hung a small oil lamp and on either side were two more charcoal censers.

'Fantastic,' the girl whispered and her voice echoed round the chamber.

'Very theatrical,' her colleague sniffed.

'But effective,' Carrington added.

'Really?' the Frenchman queried. 'I am surprised that someone as famous and down-to-earth as you should take this sort of thing seriously. What exactly is your interest?'

'Off the record?' Carrington asked and the Frenchman nodded. 'In my travels I've seen many strange and marvellous things, and if I'm certain of anything now it's that magic is a real thing. Do you know where I'm conducting my next expedition?'

'The Peruvian volcanos – we have already carried a story in our magazine.'

'So you'll know that no man has ever returned from them.'

'Fantasy,' the journalist commented.

'And my last expedition was also to a place from which no man has ever returned – the tombs of Galgatha. Do you know how I survived? I carried a charm, a talisman, which Qhe and Willard prepared for me. All I know is that it kept me safe. You can say what you like, but there were times when I should have died – and I didn't. You say that I'm down-to-earth so believe me, this is no fantasy.'

'And they will prepare another charm for this new trip of yours?' the journalist asked sarcastically.

'*He must be protected from the fire devils!*', the girl suddenly spoke and then shook her head in total bewilderment.

Her colleague laughed . . . but she frowned.

'This is a powerful room, mademoiselle,' said Qhe to the girl. 'You are tuning into reality. I am very happy for you.'

* * * * *

Qhe and Willard had changed into simple long white robes over which they wore tunics of brilliant red silk. On each of their breasts was embroidered in silver thread the insignia of the royal house of Pashman, the seven-pointed star beneath the sign of infinity.

'Now, I must ask of you only one thing: do not say a word and remain absolutely calm. Nothing will happen in this room that can harm you providing you stay where I place you and do not move.'

Qhe then guided them to an area on the opposite side of the chamber where for a space of about thirty square feet there were no mosaic patterns on the floor. Next he placed seven candles around them.

'These little flames will guard you,' he said with a smile.

'From what?' the girl asked.

'Tension,' Willard replied. 'We have to create a tension to flow through us. It is rather like placing you in an atmospherically controlled cabin.'

'But will it not harm you?'

'Qhe and I are trained for this. For instance, if you started deep sea diving you would not go lower than fifteen feet the first time – and, before that, you would have to learn how to use your equipment correctly.'

The Frenchman sniffed again.

'Judge for yourself,' Willard said kindly, 'but please don't move.'

He returned with Qhe to stand by the altar and both men fell to their knees for a minute of silent prayer.

'Only with love, only with light, only by Your Will,' Qhe chanted softly as they stood.

He then opened the cupboard under the altar and removed certain articles. With Willard aiding, he placed a cloth of shining red-orange satin on top of the altar. Having re-arranged the candles, vase, goblet and wand, he produced a block of glass in which was preserved a perfect sunflower and he placed this between the two candles. To the eyes of the three observers, it seemed to glow a luminous orange and the Frenchman blinked unsuccessfully to rid himself of the apparent hallucination. Some incense was then removed from the cupboard and simultaneously Qhe and Willard sprinkled it on to the two charcoal burners. Within a few seconds the chamber was filled with the rich warm scent of olibanum and then, within a few further seconds, the whole chamber seemed to glow with that same orange colour that had originally emanated from the sunflower in the glass.

Qhe nodded confidently to Willard and both men smiled. If they had held full control over their personal destinies, they would have chosen to spend perhaps all their time at this royal art.

'See it. Feel it,' Willard advised the three onlookers. 'This is no hallucination, believe us.'

Now Qhe removed the final object from the interior of the altar. It was wrapped in orange satin and, with infinite care and attention, he took it out from the material and let it dangle from his hand. Three inches in width, it was a pendant of perfect Ceylonese cat's eye, a black egg-shaped gem with a brilliant streak of gold running across it. He held it for a few seconds and winked at Carrington before he carefully lowered it into the gold goblet on the altar.

He then lifted up the wand, three feet long and made of white ivory with a thin thread of iron down its core, kissed it and handed it to Willard who moved to stand directly before the altar. Qhe positioned himself directly behind Willard who pointed the wand at an angle over the altar. The two men then bowed, holding their heads down for a count of ten, raised them and turned to the left. They bowed again, waited for another count of ten and then turned once more to the left. They repeated this movement twice until they were once again facing the altar.

Willard now pointed the wand upwards while Qhe placed his right hand on the Englishman's shoulder. With a confident movement that came from years of experience, Willard drew a series of occult signs in the air and, at the same time, Qhe created a resonant hum that came from deep within his chest. Willard redrew the sygils twice more and it seemed as if the tip of the wand created a silver trail through the air. Qhe intensified the vibration of the noise he was creating and the whole room seemed to quiver. Then suddenly . . . silence.

The three spectators stood with their mouths dry and their hands sweating. Whatever was happening, whatever sort of trick was being played upon them, they could feel something mysteriously and irresistibly affecting their minds and bodies.

'Ra-Hoor-Khuit,' Willard's voice broke through the silence. 'Pasht, Sekhet, Mau.'

'With love and with light,' Qhe intoned.

And both men knelt. The light orange glow that had

filled the room began to deepen creating a texture of light practically impossible to describe. It was as if the very particles of air had changed substance and colour. Qhe and Willard now hummed together that same vibrant note and a swirling vortex of silver light appeared above them, reaching up into the air through the stained glass dome and into the sky. They bowed their heads and a glistening, dancing figure moved in the silver light. The two men carefully focused the energy within their skulls a few inches behind their eyes and, as clearly as if he had stood in material form before them, they saw in their minds' eyes the golden figure of the Egyptian godling. This strange and marvellous spirit greeted them affectionately and so perfect was his understanding that he knew immediately what was desired of him.

He had no hesitation in granting the two initiates' request; it was one of the privileges that was granted them at initiation and it was truly his pleasure to so oblige them. Before doing so, however, he turned his hawk's head to look across the chamber at the three spectators and he threw them a thread of light as a blessing and gift. The two men and one woman felt themselves thrill with a strange delight, but could see nothing except the glow of mysterious luminous colours.

The spirit now returned his attention to the two initiates and placing his hand to his heart he appeared to pull from it a particle of himself. Incredibly he held in front of him an exact miniature replica of himself shining and dancing in his palm. He then signalled that the two men should lower their heads and, as they did so, he turned his palm to face them. The tiny replica broke into a million fragments that streamed down on Willard and Qhe, and the two men felt a charge of electric force shoot through them.

They waited a few more seconds while the spirit blessed them and departed, after which they knelt in gratitude. Standing again Qhe placed both his hands on his brother's shoulders, and Willard pointed his arm, making the tip of the wand touch the goblet which held the cat's eye talisman. With an effort that literally shook both men, they willed the energy that surrounded and filled them, down the wand and into the goblet.

The orange glow in the room concentrated itself and flowed down the magic weapon into the precious stone. With one further intense effort the two men broke the thin thread that connected them with the charm and Willard withdrew the wand flicking it through the air.

'Let it be,' he chanted. 'It rests. It is.'

They stepped back six steps and once more dropped to their knees. Using their minds' eyes again they cautiously probed around them. Yes, it had been done. All was correct. All was in order.

'It is done.'

'Thanks be to God.'

'With love and with light.'

Both men smiled happily and Qhe stepped forward and removed the gem from the goblet, letting it dangle from his hand. Willard meanwhile walked across the room and put out the seven candles that had helped protect the three spectators.

'You'll be safe enough in those volcanoes, James,' Qhe told the explorer. 'No fire devil will touch him now, mademoiselle.'

THREE

'Well,' Qhe asked, now that they had returned to the office on the twenty-first floor, 'what did you think?'

'I'm really extremely grateful,' Carrington replied, the cat's eye pendant already hanging from his neck.

'And you, monsieur?'

The journalist sniffed. What he had seen and felt was, to him, totally unbelievable. His mind blocked out the fact that it could have been in any way a *real* thing. It was trickery, he had decided, and yet he found himself unable to tell this to Qhe.

'I – er,' he hesitated, 'would prefer to postpone any judgement. At the very least, it was – er – extremely clever.'

'Clever, Georges!' his colleague exclaimed, her eyes burning. *'It was exceptional.'*

'You understand what happened then?' Qhe asked.

The girl started like a frightened rabbit. Everything was moving far too fast for her; new dimensions of life were being thrown at her at a speed that she could not absorb.

'No, Your Majesty,' she finally answered, 'I was referring to the photographs.'

'Of course, mademoiselle, of course,' Qhe laughed. 'And whom are you interviewing next?'

'We have not yet interviewed you,' the journalist said firmly.

'But I have nothing to say – only a few little tricks to show. Have I not done enough?'

'But you have told us nothing,' the Frenchman insisted.

'Your beautiful photographer will tell you what you want to know,' Qhe answered quickly. 'She already knew about the fire devils. She knows everything – if only she would remember.'

'Pah!' the man snorted. 'Rubbish!'

'My dear sir,' Willard now intervened, 'you have just had

the privilege of observing the King of Pashman performing a rite of ceremonial magic – surely that is an elegant sufficiency!'

The journalist frowned. Certainly he had a story, but what was frustrating him was that he sensed that there was something far larger behind it all. He was not satisfied. He wanted to know everything – *that* was his job.

'That which you want to know, monsieur,' Qhe told him, 'you will know – but only you can tell yourself.'

Normally the Frenchman would have found such words despicable, but the manner in which Qhe had said them rang such a bell of bizarre truth.

'May we see you again?' he asked politely.

'Without a doubt,' Qhe answered, 'and whom are you seeing next.'

'The three men who call themselves the Prophets of the Prophet,' the girl replied. 'They are getting an enormous following. Are they genuine?'

Qhe frowned. He had never thought about these men before, but now that he was asked he felt a strange sensation of unease. He was about to answer when the phone rang. He answered it immediately for he knew that no call would have been put through unless it was urgent.

'Yes, yes. In five minutes.'

His frown deepened. Here indeed was a weird coincidence, but he had learned long ago that there was no such thing as coincidence.

'I'm afraid that I must ask you all to leave, but if I might speak with you alone for a second, mademoiselle.'

He took the young woman's arm and led her into the next room, his private office. He opened a drawer in his desk and removed from it a small ring. It was made of silver and held the face of a strangely smiling Buddha. He took the woman's hand and placed the ring on her middle finger. She was about to blush again, thinking it a present, but the expression of deadly seriousness on Qhe's face stopped her.

'It is three thousand years old, Marie. Remember what you saw a few minutes ago and know that this ring is infinitely more powerful. When you see the three men who call themselves the Prophets of the Prophet, move close to them with this ring. Let them look at its smiling face. If they are true servers then they, too, shall smile. If they are not, they will look away. Return and tell me what happened.'

'I – I – I don't . . .'

'Believe?' he asked. 'Trust instead then.'

'But trust what?'

'You could start by trusting your belief in fire devils,' he laughed and kissed her hand. 'Do what I say and see what happens.'

He kissed her hand again and she nodded in agreement. He then escorted her to the lift and returned to the room where Willard was waiting with a stranger.

'Your Majesty,' the man said and bowed awkwardly.

'I'm delighted to meet you, Inspector. How can we help?'

The Inspector from French internal security was a thin man with slicked back black hair and a tiny pencil moustache. He stroked his moustache and then began to tell Qhe his story.

'Sir Gerald Pollinger in London suggested that you were the only man who could help us. For various reasons, my agency and others in The United States, England, Germany and Switzerland have been keeping a watch on a new quasi-religious movement, the Prophets of the Prophet. We have reason to believe that there may be something not – how shall I say – altogether savoury about them. Our best operative, Henri Marot, infiltrated one of their private meetings and has been – to put it mildly – non-operational ever since. It would seem . . .'

Qhe raised his hand to prevent the Inspector from continuing:

'We'll help.'

Less than two hours later, Qhe and the Inspector were descending from the French police helicopter into the grounds of Grenoble General Hospital. They were greeted by one of the operatives who had been in the black Citroen.

'There's no change,' he informed them. 'The psychiatrist from Paris hasn't a clue what has happened. He can't make head nor tail of it. The best he can do is to say that with time ... With time! Those bastards! We should just move in and rub them out – now – immediately.'

'We can't,' the Inspector replied gently.

'Can't? When one of our men goes down like that, then there's no *can't*.'

'In this case there is, so ...' The Inspector looked grimly at his subordinate who shut up.

They entered the main building of the hospital and Qhe wrinkled his nose at the smell of disinfectant and the rush ing nurses and doctors. This was no way to heal people – not in a factory. One day, soon, Qhe mused, humanity would relearn those old lessons about true medicine.

The tough operative sneered at Qhe's look of distaste at the hospital. Why his chief had called in this weak-willed oriental he couldn't guess for a second. This dark-skinned foreigner didn't look fit to scramble an egg let alone unscramble the mess in his comrade's brain. Qhe smiled to himself, knowing what the man was thinking, but said nothing.

They took the lift up to the third floor where a uniformed policeman stood guard. He came smartly to attention and saluted.

'Everything in order, sir.'

Qhe and the two men now moved down a long corridor and turned left into a second passage. As they entered it, Qhe suddenly raised his hand and they stopped dead.

'What the ...'

Before he could finish his sentence, a swarthy, heavily built man slid out of a doorway thirty feet away. As he saw the three men ahead of him, his eyes flashed in instant panic. Within a split second he had pulled out his revolver with its silencer. In almost the same moment, the two French security men slipped out their own pistols and dove headfirst towards the floor.

There was the deathly thud as he squeezed his trigger and the Inspector dropped his own weapon as the bullet tore through the flesh of his arm. The other operative tried to fire, but his pistol jammed and he looked up, grimacing, ready for death. But the intruder had no chance to fire again as with a horrible rattling noise he grasped at the gaping wound in his throat that had been caused by the Pashmani knife. His eyes bulged in shock and he staggered a few steps before falling forward on to his face. The tip of the knife's blade stuck out an inch and a half from the back of the man's neck.

Qhe looked calmly at the three men who lay on the floor in front of him, one of them dead, one of them wounded. He stepped forward and, looking compassionately down at the corpse, said a silent prayer. He then entered the small hospital room and grimaced at the sight of the dead doctor and nurse, and the dead man in the bed. He had not expected today to be a day of death. Normally he would have sensed what was to come – death had a scent of her very own with which Qhe was ... *too* familiar.

A few seconds later, the Inspector, grasping his flesh wound, and his colleague also entered the room.

'It seems more serious ... ' he said. 'But why?'

'Someone has a secret,' Qhe replied simply. 'Forgive me for killing that man – we might have been able to find out.'

'Forgive you, monsieur! It is we who should apologize – after all we are the professionals in this business. Without you there ...'

'Yes,' Qhe agreed, 'you would have been very professionally dead. And, yes, I'm glad that we won the first round.'

'The first round, Your Majesty?'

'Of course. Don't you feel it? Don't you feel that this is just the very beginning? We have merely taken the first step into the maze. From now on there must be infinite care. It must be played like the most sophisticated game of chess. At the slightest move, lady Death may raise her head again – lady Death and her other sinister friends. You must watch carefully to see what unfolds.'

The Inspector and his colleague both frowned and

looked with bewilderment at this strange Easterner who spoke a language whose words were foreign but whose sentiments were familiar. This gentle oriental monarch suddenly seemed infinitely dangerous.

'But I am working with you,' Qhe said, catching what they were thinking. 'The situation provides no choice.'

He gave them no time to answer, but returned to the corridor where he turned over the body of the corpse to look at the killer's face. He studied it carefully and it was an open book. The man was a gangster, someone who had been involved in crime, corruption and murder since childhood. His face held no secrets about his life; death had been its only surprise.

'A Sicilian hit-man,' the Inspector told him. 'One of their very best – they will be sad to have lost him.'

'They?' Qhe asked.

'The family – who else?'

'And he works only for the family?' Qhe queried.

'Only for Don Gillamo – as far as we know.'

Qhe's face broke into a wide grin at the mention of Gillamo's name. Providence certainly had a few pleasant tricks up her slippery sleeve. His smile broadened until he was actually chuckling.

'You know the man?' the Inspector asked.

'No, not yet,' Qhe answered, 'but I have a date to see him tomorrow afternoon – to buy something, something very important.'

'May I ask what,Your Majesty?'

'Certainly. I'm going to buy a gem, the Palermo diamond – for my son.'

'For your son?'

'For whom else?' Qhe exclaimed. 'I'm making him a bull – I need the diamond for one of the bull's eyes. You see, my child is a Taurus and he needs his talisman.'

'But with the Palermo diamond? That is worth millions of francs and Gillamo would never sell it. For a bull!'

'But, of course,' Qhe laughed and took the Inspector's arm to lead him down the corridor. 'Do you believe in magic?'

'In night club acts,' came the cynical answer.

'Well, before this is over you'll see it on a larger stage. May I see your files on all this?' Qhe asked, suddenly changing the subject, his voice now deadly serious.

The Frenchman immediately pulled himself away from Qhe and frowned.

'Your Majesty,' he answered very slowly and hesitantly, 'this is a police matter, a matter of national security. We have no provisions for civilians to be involved. You came here to help us on one particular thing and that thing – that man – is now dead. I'm sorry,' he shrugged, 'but . . .'

Qhe sighed and again smiled to himself. He then looked coldly into the man's eyes.

'You little human beings can still amaze me. You have eyes, but you never see. You open the door for me to help and then you close it.'

The Frenchman trembled at the coldness of Qhe's words. There was no anger or fury in them, just an icy ring of truth. He tried to look away from Qhe's gaze, but his eyes were held rigid like a rabbit with a cobra.

'When you ask again,' Qhe said, 'I will still say yes, but this affair is already too big for you, too big for you and your comrades across the globe.'

He now looked away and the poor man had to shake his head to regain clear consciousness.

'I am still grateful,' he stuttered.

'That I killed someone for you?' Qhe responded and began to walk away.

FOUR

'It's a pretty nauseating partnership,' Willard told Qhe. 'The Prophets of the Prophet Movement and the Mafia or whatever you fancy calling it. It's just about the finishing touch to the whole disgusting business. We should have taken a look years ago, shouldn't we? How we didn't notice them is beyond me. Take a look at this for a start.'

He passed Qhe a sheet of typewritten figures.

'What is it?'

'Estimated income of the movement over the last two years.'

Qhe looked at the sheet of paper and whistled. The figures were truly enormous. He then looked at the *top secret* stamp across the top of the paper and chuckled.

'From Paris?' he asked.

'An old friend,' Willard answered casually. 'One of our brethren in the Ministry owed a favour and spent a few minutes photocopying.'

'A few minutes!' Qhe exclaimed, looking at the thick sheaf of papers. 'What exactly do we have there?'

'For starters, they don't have the connection with the underworld. But there're a few things that make really tasty reading.'

Qhe laughed at the way his old friend rolled the word *tasty*. Willard's impeccable English gentleman's accent gave it a certain indefinable style.

'Dear, dear brother,' Qhe smiled, 'what are we getting into this time?'

'The usual torrid nastiness,' Willard winked back. 'Firstly, the Prophets have about half a million adherents scattered across the globe – my feeling is that these people are almost incidental to the main core of the movement, which the French estimate at about two thousand. The majority of these two thousand are from the Arab countries and Iran, and – and this is the first big point – too many of them are senior men involved in controlling, and owning, oil money. Lots of money, therefore – lots and lots and lots of lolly.'

'How much?'

'Enough to make international currency dealing look like snakes and ladders,' Willard sniffed. 'Now then, big point number two is that every man that's been infiltrated into the central group of the movement has come out totally unhinged. Some haven't come out at all, but have stayed in to help the Prophets.'

'And the man I was supposed to help?' Qhe asked.

'An exception to the rule perhaps.' Willard answered. 'Strong enough to hold a part of his mind intact – they must have been afraid that he'd rebalance himself and start talking. But let's move on to big point number three and this, really, is peculiarly bizarre. Of the two thousand people that were surmised to be part of the central core, three hundred of them have died – withered away from a new form of cancer.'

'No medical theories?'

'None at all. The whole movement could be seen as one great cancerous growth, couldn't it?' Willard sighed and threw down the sheaf of papers. 'What's really niggling me is all that money.'

'All that money and Don Gillamo,' Qhe added. 'They're going to do something with it.'

'Certainly,' Willard replied. 'Get very very rich.'

Qhe smiled sadly and shook his head.

'Why is it,' he finally said, 'that every time we start getting involved, I just want to go back to Pashman and sit chanting in the temple with my son sitting between my knees?'

'With me hitting a gong behind you, eh?'

Both men laughed and looked gently into each other's eyes. In their ancient brotherhood and friendship, they found a tranquil strength that never failed to reassure – the king of the small paradise in the Himalayas and the impeccable Englishman. Initiate magicians and priests, they could have asked for nothing more from life other than to be able to spend their time weaving their magic of white light in beautiful ceremonial rite and prayer, but their paths did not allow this.

For Qhe there had been no choice at all. From the very moment that he was born he had been destined to become a warrior for light on the physical plane. In the twentieth century, it was no longer sufficient for the monarch of Pashman to lead his countrymen in prayer to balance the world's energies for humanity as the Pashmanis had done for over four thousand years. His duties lay elsewhere from the sparkling emerald green valley in the mountains between India and Tibet. Willard, however, had had a choice, but his karmic tie to Qhe had been so great that he had not thought twice about joining and serving with his brother. And certainly, over the last few years, if one thing had been proved: it was that they *were* needed. From the moment that they had stolen the three nuclear warheads, from France, Russia and the United States, in order to ensure non-interference from the superpowers, Qhe and Willard had been continuously involved in a strange warfare of sorcery. It was as if planet Earth were going through some tumultuous illness which heralded a total cure in the near future, but that poisonous ulcers kept erupting on her surface which needed lancing and healing. With magic, prayer and other more ordinary weapons, Qhe and his brother Willard were the leading healers.

Qhe looked at his watch and frowned.

'I have to leave in a minute to visit our Sicilian friend. Play it by ear, don't you think?'

'By ear,' Willard agreed. 'And I'll do a bit more nosing around on this money. And, of course, our journalist friends will soon be with the Prophets – that will prove interesting.'

'Too interesting perhaps,' Qhe answered. 'Too interesting by far.'

In the entrance hall to the chateau near Grenoble, the two journalists, Georges Purot and Marie de Baldeau, were greeted by two young men with sweet welcoming smiles but deeply suspicious eyes.

'I'm sorry but Mademoiselle must leave her cameras with us for safe-keeping – they'll be quite all right.' The young man's voice was as treacley as his smile and held just the slightest hint of a threat.

Marie was about to protest, but it had taken months to set up this interview and photographs could always be taken later. She nodded demurely and handed over her equipment.

'And if you would now care to remove your shoes . . .'

Georges Purot had some difficulty in refraining from sneering at this request, but he kept his face straight and knelt to undo his laces. Never in all his years in journalism had he had so much difficulty with a story. A twenty-page feature on occultism and mysticism! Give Purot a nice straight-forward war, famine or riot anytime! Right now it seemed to him as if the whole world was inhabited by freaks, but . . . but he was a professional and, as a professional, he would do his job and do it well.

'May I keep my notebook?' he asked carefully.

The two young men looked at each other for a few seconds. Could a notebook cause any harm?

'You may,' one of them finally answered.

Purot gave the man a grateful nod. Although this seasoned and hardened journalist would have sneered at all the mystic rubbish, yet he had certain respect for the Prophet of Prophets and other similar movements. Purot had an understanding and respect for power – in whatever form it came – and he knew that these strange groups did have power: power in controlling people and power in money. A political or nationalistic party he could understand, but it was the motives behind these freak religious movements that bemused him. Yes, he would let his photographer hand over her cameras and, yes, he would remove his shoes. He would put up with all this pretentious sensitivity to get his story.

'You are allowed to see them now.'

Purot and Marie were led down a series of corridors to a

room at the rear of the chateau. As they walked, they let their journalists' noses sniff out the atmosphere. It was a peculiar scent, a strange atmosphere, that they caught. Though everything seemed calm enough, there was something in it that was not quite safe, something that kept the muscles in one's stomach continuously tense.

They reached a set of huge double doors and stopped.

'You understand,' one of the men said, 'that they have little time and that this is a great honour – a very great honour – for you.'

Purot nodded.

'How did you both come to work with them?' he suddenly asked.

The two young men's eyes flashed for a brief second like frightened rabbits' and then they looked at Purot as if his question had been totally meaningless.

'Well?' he insisted very gently.

Their eyes went blank. They could not understand his question. It raised concepts that were beyond their grasp, concepts which made them feel wounded and angry. He had no right to interfere with them like this.

Both Purot and Marie sensed the immediate change in their feeling and stance. That simple question had provoked complete and hysterical hostility. Purot decided to try once more, but stopped before the words crossed his lips, feeling suddenly that just one more tiny probe would push them over the brink.

'Excuse me,' he said ingratiatingly, 'you have been very kind to us all along. May we go in?'

'A great honour,' the words were whispered back at him. 'Remember a great honour.'

As all this took place, Marie became aware of a peculiar tingling sensation upon one of her fingers. She remembered the ring that Qhe had given her. She had thought it a childish practical joke since leaving Qhe in Marseilles, but now it seemed to hold some true reality. She realized that she was holding her arms crossed in front of her and that the tiny Buddha face was smiling directly at the two young men. She felt completely self-conscious and foolish as she slowly uncrossed her arms and placed her hands behind her back. Within seconds the atmosphere had eased and the two ushers had relaxed.

'We felt called to their service,' one of them now cleanly answered Purot's question and wiped away a bead of sweat from his brow.

'How?' Purot asked.

'It is a long story,' came the polite but evasive response. 'You must now go in. Please.'

The double doors were swung open and they entered. As in Qhe's chamber, the room was filled with the odour of incense, but it was a smell that was completely different. Instead of calming the body and mind, it made them thrill with an uneasy excitement. So powerful was its effect that it was several seconds before Purot and Marie were sufficiently adjusted to focus on the room. It was dimly lit except for one area on the opposite side where, shoulder by shoulder and in their different coloured robes, stood the three men who called themselves the Prophets of the Prophet.

'Come, come, we welcome you,' the Persian said proffering his hand. 'We shall not stand on ceremony.'

'We are your brothers – nothing more, nothing less,' the Japanese added.

A shiver of panic ran up Marie's spine as she realized that she would have to shake hands with these men – shake with her right hand. They would feel her ring, *the* ring. To the three prophets it looked as if she was shyly dithering beside the door, wringing her hands nervously behind her. They were correct about her nervousness, but the wringing of her hands – she was frantically trying to pull the ring off the middle finger of her right hand.

It was a close fit and the more she pulled the more it seemed to catch in the fold of her skin. Her palms began to sweat and the ring suddenly dropped off clinking on the wooden floor. Without hesitation she dropped to her knees to retrieve it and Purot turned round amazed at what he took to be a sign of devotion to the three Prophets. His eyes narrowed, however, as he saw her pick up the ring and push it on to her left hand. Luckily his own body had blocked the prophets' view of her and they, too, thought that she was merely demonstrating her devotion.

'Not necessary, not necessary,' the European in his purple robes told her, 'but charming, very charming.'

She staggered to her feet, straightened her jacket and trousers, and moved forward to stand beside Purot who, althought tempted, said nothing. They stepped forward together and shook the hands of the Prophets whose grips were limp and fishlike; Purot immediately noted this.

'We have no need to show our strength, Monsieur Purot,' the Japanese told him.

'Anyone,' the Persian continued, 'can shake hands firmly and show himself to be strong.'

'You do not need to show this?' Purot asked.

'We do not,' the European answered. 'We may show it in other ways.'

'How?'

'The future will tell, Monsieur Purot. You will see.'

'What exactly shall I see?'

'The coming,' came the simple answer, 'but shall we take tea first.'

They now walked to a tiny ante-room which held a small octagonal table with five chairs around it. They sat down and a young man with a scar across his forehead and a squint entered bearing a tea tray. Having placed it upon the table, he left the room backwards, cringing and bowing.

'This,' the Japanese said to Purot and Marie, 'is the civilized way for you to come to understand us.'

As he said this, he shot them both a look of such intensity that they immediately looked away. As they looked away, they caught the eyes of the other two Prophets and they too stared back at them with the same intensity. For almost a minute the table was completely silent. Marie held herself mentally together by thinking only of the ring on her finger and Purot had also to reorient his mind which he did by thinking around the fact that these men – whatever else they were – were certainly master hypnotists.

'Only by knowing us,' the Persian said, 'can you understand us.'

'Only by seeing can you believe,' intoned the Japanese.

'Only through belief comes knowledge.'

'Through knowledge comes power.'

'Through power comes God.'

'From God come His Prophets.'

'One is yet to come.'

'He who has come before shall return.'

'We herald him!'

And then again there was silence which was broken only by the Japanese asking with great politeness:

'Does Mademoiselle take sugar in her tea?'

She nodded and deep inside her something wanted to scream. The atmosphere was claustrophobic and heavy beyond belief. She looked to Purot who was now sweating.

'Yes, it's very hot in here,' the European apologized and then smiled cunningly. 'Sometimes we have difficulty in controlling the temperature. A joke, you understand? A joke.'

Purot managed to raise a feeble smile. Everything was beginning to hold a dreamlike quality for him. He frowned and massaged his forehead. A dream, he said to himself, no, more like a nightmare. Then, without warning, he felt himself relaxing and beginning to feel stronger. Marie had placed her hand on his wrist and the ring was touching his bare flesh.

'Tell me how this all started?' he asked firmly.

The three Prophets stared back and there was now a look of fury in their faces. Their eyes narrowed and they looked with fierce intensity at this man who was not falling under their spell.

'Come now, gentlemen,' he continued. 'no more eye games please. Let us conduct this in a civilized manner.'

Purot was surprised at his own words. They carried a strength and sincerity that was almost foreign.

'As you yourselves say,' he went on, 'seeing is believing. So far I see nothing.'

A war of dangerous psychic wills had begun and Purot felt his mind starting to split in two: one part of him, strong and secure, ready to squash these men; the other part wanting only to crumble to the floor, give in completely and kiss their feet. Marie felt herself to be moving into something resembling a trance and yet in this trance all was more real than anything in her life so far. She closed her eyes and could still see everything only there was more colour. Around the three prophets was a dull grey-green cloud with flashes of red and purple. She focused down at the ring which shone the most brilliant gold and rose. And she looked at her colleague, Purot, whose body was surrounded by a volcano of changing colours as he attempted to deflect the three Prophets malicious evil energies.

Suddenly she knew what she had to do. There was no choice in the matter as she realized the horrible blackness that confronted her. Without warning she stood up and held out her hand, making the small Buddha face smile out at the prophets. Instantly the three men winced and seemed almost transfixed.

'We're leaving,' she whispered to Purot, 'leaving now.'

Her colleague was not for one second going to argue and he stood immediately. As they began to back away from the table, the three Prophets began to move menacingly towards them.

'Come close enough,' she hissed her warning, 'and I shall touch you with this ring.'

Saying this, she willed a beam of light to strike out from it to them and, again, they stopped rigid.

'Do not move,' she repeated vehemently. 'Not a step!'

She and Purot backed slowly out of the room, through the main room and into the corridor. She slammed the double doors shut and then, acting totally instinctively, made the sign of the pentagram against it. Now, and only now, did they begin running down the corridor. As they reached the main hallway, the two ushers who had originally met them, appeared to block their way. All the fury and anger that Purot had felt against the three Prophets erupted against these two men as, filled with the strength of a madman, he hurled them aside and against the walls.

Less than fifteen seconds later, their car was skidding

across the gravel of the driveway and out on to the open road. Inside the chateau, the three Prophets immersed in their stinking murky cloud, realized that the time had come to behave less gently.

FIVE

Don Gillamo, cigar in his mouth and wearing only a pair of leopard skin swimming briefs, lay comfortably back in his reclining chair while two young blondes in bikinis manicured his hands and a redhead massaged his massive hairy shoulders. On the video screen in front of him he was watching for the thirty-seventh time *The Godfather Part Two* and chuckling to himself. Yes indeed, he like the way the young godfather kept promising his wife that the family's affairs were going to become legal, strictly legitimate. What a joke!

A red light flashed over the screen and Gillamo withdrew his right hand from one of the blondes and pressed a button on a control panel at his side. The picture on the screen flickered and the image gave way to a view of the front gate to his estate, where a longbase white Rolls-Royce was drawing up outside. The driver was a young Pashmani boy, just seventeen and dressed in white robes. At his side was a younger boy similarly dressed and in the rear, reading a comic and reclining on the white upholstery, was Qhe in a white silk suit and a huge straw hat pulled down over his forehead. He was deeply involved in his Marvelman comic in which the hero was currently dealing with a monster spider from outer space.

Qhe knew full well that they had drawn up at the estate's gates and he could guess that they were already being watched, but he had his act well thought out and he wanted to play this man, Gillamo, like a master angler with a tadpole.

Gillamo, still in his chair, operated the camera into close-up of his visitor and smiled. At the very least this would make for an interesting afternoon. He had heard rumours about this man, Qhe, but nothing really solid except that he was worthy of respect. Gillamo had no intention of selling the Palermo diamond, but it would be of interest to see how much would be offered for it. Two of his men now appeared on the screen to identify the guests, but Gillamo flicked another switch.

'Let them in,' he ordered into the microphone.

His voice suddenly echoed out from two hidden speakers at the gate, but even now Qhe did not look up for one second from his comic. Gillamo rose, put on a satin dressing gown that he once belonged to Muhammed Ali and went to greet his visitor.

As the car stopped in front of the huge villa's main entrance, Qhe did not hurry but carefully flicked through the few remaining pages of his comic before sighing, placing it down at his side and casually climbing out of the car as one of his boys opened the door. He looked slowly up the steps to the barrel-chested man in the satin dressing gown and then, with infinite politeness and grace, removed his straw hat and bowed.

'Yes, it is so pleasant to go visiting on a beautiful afternoon like this,' he said languidly.

'Sure, sure,' Gillamo answered enthusiastically, 'nothing better in the world.'

The Don was suddenly embarrassed by his own speediness. The slowness of Qhe made him look like a gibbering chipmonk.

'Please come in,' he said very slowly.

'You're kind, very kind,' Qhe answered. 'The heat – it makes me feel so casual.'

It was now that Don Gillamo realized that his guest was posing.

'Of course, Your Majesty. Naturally, Your Majesty,' he said getting into the mood of it. 'Allow me to help you.'

He took Qhe's arm and play-acted helping him into the house. Gillamo was truly amused. It had been many years since he had met someone with whom he could play, someone of equal strength and position.

'We respect each other, huh?' he asked, still holding Qhe's arm.

'Of course, my friend,' Qhe answered, but his voice was

now crisp and he gave Don Gillamo a wink.

Inside himself, however, he was shuddering at the man's intimate touch for Qhe had always been sensitive to one thing: *psychic filth.*

They entered the huge lounge and Qhe quickly took in its rich vulgarity with its two-inch deep carpeting, the alcove with the snooker table, the full-length bar, the rare paintings that were hung only for their financial value and the thirty yard long window that looked out across the piano-shaped swimming pool with its half-dozen bikinied and failed starlets, and the two men in their sharkskin suits with bulges under the armpits.

'A nice room,' he said approvingly, 'and your paintings are extremely good.'

'Just a place for the summer,' Gillamo answered deprecatingly. 'It's quiet enough. You wanna drink?'

Qhe nodded and Gillamo pressed a button. Within seconds, one of the blondes who had been manicuring him sidled into the room, pouting and swinging her hips and everything else. She slid up to Gillamo and looked up at him as if he were Hercules.

'My usual, sweetheart,' he told her. 'And for you, Qhe?'

'A fresh orange juice will be fine,' Qhe answered.

Gillamo raised his eyebrows, but then shrugged tolerantly, gave the blonde a pat on her behind to set her moving. She pouted once more before going to the bar.

'A swim?' the Don asked, but Qhe shook his head.

The two men received their glasses and then stood five yards apart carefully looking at each other. Qhe did not need to stare – one glance at the man had been sufficient. He was as hard as nails, clever, with a sophisticated animal cunning, ruthless, totally cruel and without conscience. He took his own animal pleasures extremely seriously as he took his business, the business of criminal money. To say that he was evil in Qhe's mind would not have been correct. To Qhe, Gillamo was a highly developed slug with tentacles made up of bullets and dollar bills.

The expression, however, on Qhe's face was impassive as he watched and allowed Gillamo to look him carefully over. And Gillamo was impressed. He was impressed first by the fact that Qhe was rich, stinking rich. Secondly because he was in good trim physical shape. And thirdly because he was cool. The big question mark in the shrewd Sicilian's mind was just how much of a fellow criminal this oriental monarch was. Was he here just about the diamond or was he playing another game?

'So you want the diamond,' he finally said.

Qhe nodded.

'And nothing else?'

Qhe shrugged non-comittally. Gillamo was about to say something when the phone rang. He moved across the room with an agility surprising for his size.

'Yes,' he answered sharply and then remained silent as one of his aides, who had been watching the scene in the lounge on the hidden closed circuit video system, told him that he recognized Qhe.

'He's the man,' Gillamo was told, 'who hit our man in the hospital.'

'You're certain?'

'Are there two people like that down this part of France?'

'Are you certain?' Gillamo repeated very coldly.

'Yes, I'm sure,' the aide answered quietly.

Gillamo put his little finger in his mouth to clean a tooth and slowly replaced the phone in its cradle. He turned equally slowly and, still picking his teeth, frowned and looked at Qhe. Qhe bowed graciously – it would have taken a fool not to know what Gillamo had just been told.

'I'm sorry,' Qhe said, 'but I just happened to be there and, you know, he might have killed me.'

'And I might have been happy.'

'I doubt it.'

There was a silence. Qhe waited patiently for Gillamo's reaction and only hoped that it would be an easy one to play against. The Sicilian looked at his guest, the man who had killed one of his best torpedos, without saying a word and then walked over to the bar where he lit a huge cigar. He inhaled deeply and, as he did so, he felt the anger rising within him. A member of his family had been killed – he did not care how or for what good reason – and he wanted, he needed revenge. And now the killer, the murderer of his relative, was a guest in his own house. Standing coolly there, sipping at his orange juice, standing on his carpet, in his home!

Qhe felt his own stomach beginning to tense in an invisible rapport with his host and knew that the situation was approaching danger level. Still holding his glass and not moving, Qhe centred his consciousness in his skull, held it there a few seconds and then centred in on his throat. A few seconds later, he gently concentrated on his heart and then created a swirling triangle of energy between the three points. When it was moving smoothly, he gradually lowered the energy into his solar plexus where it had an immediate calming effect and then willed it across the room to Don Gillamo.

Gillamo began to relax and took a more gentle drag on his cigar. Come on, he told himself, his man had been a fool to get caught. This was no time to start getting sentimental. Hell, it meant he had even more respect for his guest. At least this white-suited oriental pansy could look after himself.

'You're pretty hot with a knife, huh?'

'When needed. Don Gillamo, I do apologize.'

'It's nothing, nothing. He'd done what he had to do. If you'd killed him before that, it would have been a different matter. But listen, what were you doing there?'

'The French police seemed to think I'm something of an expert on religion and magic.'

'Hocus pocus, and bullshit,' Gillamo laughed, 'if the Vatican didn't own so many banks, I'd think they were weird too.'

He roared with laughter at his own joke and Qhe applauded approvingly, but the laughter was suddenly cut off by Gillamo's question:

'And what are you doing here?'

'I want to buy the Palermo diamond – for my son, his first birthday present.'

'Don't give me that garbage, Qhe. If you've got any

respect for me, show it, but don't give me garbage.'

'Believe me, that is one of my reasons.'

'Well, it's not for sale. Never. I'm just seeing you out of curiosity, but now,' he shrugged, 'it looks like maybe you've got another reason.'

'I do want that diamond. Before his birthday,' Qhe smiled, 'I'm sure you'll sell it.'

'Of course, of course,' Gillamo bellowed and slapped his thigh, 'I'll sell it to you the same day the Pope gives communion to the King of Saudi Arabia.'

'Is that so far off?' Qhe answered sweetly.

There was another silence through which Qhe retained his sweet smile.

'I'll tell you what I also want, Don Gillamo – shall I?'

'Go ahead, tell me. You expect the mountain to come to you?'

'I want you first to understand that what I'm doing is very rare. Usually things like this do not interest me . . . you are the head of a business concern, a very big concern admittedly, but I am the monarch of a country – I own a kingdom. You are the head of a family, the chief executive of a company, but I am a king. You have your men, but I have an army. You own a chief of police or a minister, but I can dine with the President. I respect you – you respect me. *I want a slice of the Prophets*!'

He said it so gently and as if it made so much sense that Gillamo was in no position to raise even a look of surprise. Fifteen seconds later, he had recovered himself.

'You mean those freakolas that that policeman we hit had just been to see. You're making a big mistake – our interest in that policeman was an ancient vendetta, it had nothing to do with those weirdos.'

'Garbage,' Qhe whispered. 'Please, Don Gillamo, don't give me garbage.'

Gillamo had no time to answer before the phone in the room rang again.

'Look, I said no calls. Who? Okay, okay, put him through. What? Who? How come? How the hell did they get in there? Invited? Yeah. Sure, sure. No, nothing. Soon!

Very soon!'

He slammed down the receiver and swore vehemently to himself in Italian. He aggressively stubbed out his quarter smoked cigar and lit another.

'You'll forgive me a second,' he said to Qhe, 'I have a little business to attend to.'

'You won't find the two journalists,' Qhe told him quietly. He said it with the assurance of a man who held every trump up his sleeve and now that he knew for certain about the so-called Prophets, the ballgame had moved right into his court. Silently, he thanked the gods for the timing of that phone call.

Gillamo spun round and, scowling viciously, looked at Qhe.

'I could rub you out here and now.'

Qhe shrugged nonchalantly.

'I still want a slice of the Prophets of the Prophet. I just don't think you'll be able to continue without me.'

'Without your protection!' Gillamo answered, his voice rising. 'You talk to me like I'm running some delicatessen which you'll burn down!'

Again, Qhe shrugged.

'A slice of the cake, Gillamo. It makes sense to do business with me. With my connections the business could expand, really expand. If I take something, I give something. You won't lose, believe me. I don't play children's games. If you want more later, you take less now – or, maybe, you take nothing.'

'I should squash you like a fly against a window!' Gillamo screamed.

'Be reasonable, Don Gillamo, this is only business.'

'On your terms! Nobody comes to me – to my family – on their terms! Who the hell are you? What do I know about you? I don't even know what side of the fence you're on. You don't even –'

'– I'll make you *more* money,' Qhe said insistently, looking deep into the Sicilian's eyes. 'Believe me, trust me.'

'Trust you?' Gillamo shouted. 'Trust a stranger?'

'I'll even do you a favour,' Qhe said smiling.

'A favour?'

'A favour after which we'll talk again. I'm not an impatient or an ungrateful man. The two journalists – let me take them on a little trip for you. Just for starters, let me kill them for you. To show good will, you understand. I'll even do it myself.'

Gillamo's face calmed somewhat. At the very least it gave him some time.

'One of my boys with you at the time?' he asked. 'With you when you do it?'

'But of course,' Qhe answered, bowing politely. 'I'll kill them in front of an orchestra at a wedding party if you like.'

Gillamo's mouth twisted into the semblance of a smile at Qhe's macabre humour.

'Sure,' Gillamo finally answered, 'why not? What better way of starting business?'

SIX

Going up in the lift of the International Gems building, Qhe tried unsuccessfully to ignore the stink of cheap after-shave on the gorilla whom Gillamo had placed at his side to watch the killings. The man was huge and fat, his stomach rolling over the belt on his trousers and he chewed gum incessantly at the same time as a cigarette hung continually from the corner of his moving mouth.

'Dis whole place yours, huh?' the hoodlum asked in an accent that was a mixture of Naples and Chicago.

Qhe nodded painfully.

'Pretty smart deal you got going then. I always – uh – you know – appreciated a tasty setup. And dis is tasty – supremo tasty numero uno.'

Qhe winced at the man's words and turned slowly to face him. He was not normally an impolite man, but this psychopathic ape – albeit a younger brother – did not deserve his politeness.

'I tell you one thing,' Qhe said quietly. 'You shut up or when I top the two journalists, there might be another passenger on their one-way trip.'

To emphasize his meaning, he gave the man a deep look and then drew his finger across his throat at the same time making a hideous rattling noise. He did it so coldly that the cheap hoodlum knew that it was no joke.

'Sure, sure,' he agreed urgently, lighting another cigarette and pushing a third piece of gum into his mouth.

The lift stopped on the twenty-first floor and they walked immediately to his main office where Willard, with some papers, was waiting for him. The Englishman looked up suspiciously at Qhe's companion.

'The deal's being sewn up,' Qhe said.

Willard's look of suspicion deepened at Qhe's new manner of speech.

'Oh really,' he answered as poshly as he possibly could.

'Class, real class,' the hoodlum could not prevent himself from saying.

Qhe's eyes rolled upwards to heaven in silent prayer.

'Shall I?' Willard asked.

'Please, please,' Qhe replied.

'Come here, young man,' Willard ordered the gangster in a crisp schoolmaster's voice.

'What?' the hoodlum answered.

'Get your ass over here, you fat ape,' Willard repeated the command in more understandable language.

Automatically, the hoodlum's hand moved towards his gun, but he was stopped. He found something irresistibly fascinating about the Englishman's eyes; it seemed as if they were infinitely deep pools into which he could fall like a pebble into a well.

'Now come here,' Willard repeated gently.

In total trance, the man obeyed the order until he was standing a few feet away from Willard who raised his hands and placed them on either side of the man's skull.

'Gently going under,' Willard said insistently. 'Under, under, under. You will hear nothing, see nothing unless we tell you. Nothing at all unless we tell you. Under, under, under.'

The gangster was now perfectly in a deep hypnotic trance and he stood there, rigid, catatonic.

'Could you put him somewhere else?' Qhe asked. 'He doesn't really fit the decor.'

'Of course,' Willard replied and, taking the gangster's arm, led him like a child to a corner of the room where he left him facing the wall.

'The journalists are here?' Qhe now asked.

'Yes, they came immediately. They're still pretty shaken, but they're both tough. The girl, Marie, is quite a brave little warrior and pretty with it. She's able to accept it mentally with little difficulty, but Purot . . . well, he's just confused and pretending not to be.'

'I have to kill them, you know,' Qhe stated blandly.

'With that gorilla as a witness? Shall we get it over with

now then? I've some more papers and information on the Prophets which is very interesting.'

'Good, good. Yes, we might as well do it now and get it out of the way,' Qhe answered as casually as ever. 'Will you get them in?'

Willard left the room and Qhe stood there, humming to himself and looking out of the window at the glorious view across Marseilles and the Mediterranean. Yes, he mused, this was all turning out to be a fascinating case. Everything appeared to be neatly falling together and it would not be long now before they could move in to deal with the Prophets. Prophets indeed! he laughed. Just three unpleasant men who somehow or other had become adepts at the Black Arts and were exceptionally greedy. Gillamo, on the other hand, could be dealt with by a five-year-old Pashmani boy blindfold and with both hands tied behind his back – though it would be pleasant to neutralize the whole of Gillamo's family. He then turned to look at the back of the gangster who was still standing in the room's corner. His classroom dunce's situation evoked Qhe's sympathy, but, Qhe thought, standing like that for a few hundred years would do him some good.

The door opened and Qhe turned to greet Marie and Purot. They looked tired and nervous, and yet in the girl's eyes there was a hint of great excitement.

'Your first experience of this kind?' Qhe asked kindly.

'What kind?' Purot replied aggressively.

'A new dimension, a separate reality,' Qhe answered simply. 'The rules are very different on this side of the fence, but you, mademoiselle, you have experienced this before, have you not? It is not so unfamiliar to you. It rings bells of truth that you recognize, does it not?'

She looked at him, her mind once again splitting into that strange duality. One part of her wanted to scream *no*, the other wanted coolly to agree with him.

'The more you experience it,' Qhe said, 'the more your confusion will disappear. Believe me, it is a real thing.'

'But what is?' she asked. 'What is a real thing?'

Twenty-five years old, dressed in blue denim jeans and

shirt, her hair held back in a pony tail, Marie de Baldeau looked every part the liberated twentieth-century career woman. For the last few years her whole life had been orientated to becoming a successful news photographer. She had learned how to hustle her way through the media world, to stay cold and impassive as she focused her camera on any situation, and was now beginning to get a reputation. Editors were starting to actually ask for her work and she was almost continuously on assignment. This was all that she wanted and all that mattered to her. But suddenly she had been thrown into a situation that was shattering every one of her concepts. She had found a part of herself that knew things she could never remember learning, that made her behave in a way that was foreign and familiar at the same time. It would all have been totally crazy – completely insane – except that she was also confronted by a man, Qhe, who seemed to make it all absolutely normal.

'Exciting, isn't it?' Qhe suddenly said and she nodded in agreement only then to shake her head.

Qhe laughed.

'And I'm afraid that I have to kill you now.'

His voice cut through the room and the two journalists froze. Purot looked immediately for an escape, but instinctively the girl held up the little Buddha ring to face Qhe. Again, he laughed.

'For our other guest's sake, you understand. I wouldn't dream of doing it just for myself and, of course, it would be extremely helpful if you'd co-operate.'

'From one crazy house,' Purot spat, 'to another. I know there is no escape, but to co-operate in my own death! I spit on you!'

Qhe frowned and a look of infinite concern crossed his face.

'My dear sir,' Qhe said, 'you must understand that if you do not die now then your lives will be in great great danger.'

'Get on with it!' Purot replied.

Marie now knew for certain that she had entered a

complete dream world. Qhe was threatening to kill her and yet she felt no fear – he was lying.

'I shall do it now.'

'Very well,' Willard sighed.

The Englishman moved to the corner of the room and gently turned round the hoodlum. To Purot and Marie, the man's expression was horribly sinister – he looked like the meanest zombie they had ever encountered.

'You hear me?' Willard asked and the hood nodded. 'Good. You are now going to watch the two journalists being brutally murdered. All right?'

The man nodded again.

'You will listen,' Willard told him, 'and believe what Qhe is about to say and show you.'

'Are you watching, gorilla? I am now kicking mademoiselle in the stomach.'

In absurd slow motion, Qhe turned and lifted his right foot in a simulated donkey kick into Marie's stomach. His foot stopped a good two feet away from her.

'It thuds into her,' Qhe continued, 'and she falls to the ground groaning and in agony.'

The hoodlum's face smiled distantly – he liked it.

'The man, Purot,' Qhe went on, 'now comes to protect her, but my hand chops across his neck and he falls heavily on top of her. Look! I am kicking them both. They are writhing in agony. What fun we're all having!'

The hoodlum's tranced face nodded in appreciative recognition of what was happening; every word that Qhe described, he could see in full and absolute reality. When Qhe said that he was standing on the girl's wrist to break it, the hood could hear the breaking of the bones. When Qhe told him that the girl was screaming in unbearable frightened pain, his ear drums vibrated to the noise of her yell of terror. It was described to him how Purot was attempting a comeback only to be kicked viciously in the teeth.

For over two minutes, the scene of torture was meticulously described in every detail. Marie stood back by the window now suppressing a flood of giggles that was attempting to overcome her and even Purot was beginning to smile wryly. Willard merely sat down behind a desk with a look of infinite boredom on his face.

'And now, gorilla,' Qhe continued, 'look! There is a gun in my hand. The man and the woman are looking up at me, their eyes pathetically pleading to be spared. I fire once.' He paused to allow the hood to imagine the sound of the report. 'But it was aimed between the man's legs. He is now whimpering. I fire again.' Again, he paused. 'The bullet hits the girl's kneecap. She screams. I fire a bullet into the man's skull. I fire a second bullet into the girl's skull. It is over – all over. I smile happily down at the work that I have finished. Okay?'

'Good, good,' the gangster grunted.

Willard sighed wearily and rose from behind the desk to take the man's arm and to lead him off to the lift.

'I am now going to release you from your trance. When awake, you shall remember coming here and you shall remember the gruesome perfection of the two murders. It will all be totally alive to you in your normal life. You will remember nothing about the trance. You will remember every detail of Qhe killing the man and woman. Is that understood?'

The gangster nodded and Willard took the man's head between his hands and blew gently into his eyes. Within seconds, the eyes began to unglaze and normal consciousness regained control.

'Okay?' Willard asked.

'Sure,' the hood answered. 'Dat was a pretty neat job. The king did it with style. Like I said, that's what I always like about a man – style. Tasty, very tasty.'

'So go and tell Gillamo that everything's fine.'

The hood lit a cigarette and put a stick of chewing gum in his mouth. He inhaled heavily, his mouth dropped to one side and he looked long and cold at Willard.

'Yeah, I'll tell the Don that everything went fine. But first, there's just one other thing that I have to do.'

The man was an ape. He signalled his move with such obviousness that it would have taken a total idiot not to recognize what he was planning. The thing that gave him such brainless confidence was Willard's English appearance of weak harmlessness.

His hand moved to his shoulder holster and his confidence was increased by the way Willard just calmly and innocently kept watching. He slowly removed the gun and pointed it at Willard's skull.

'You didn't really think the Don would let you get away with this sort of crap, did you?' he sneered. 'It don't show sufficient respect. You're playing with professionals, buster, real professionals. You and your fancy friend, you –'

His words were abruptly and brutally cut off as Willard lashed forward. In a movement that lasted a split second, the Englishman's left hand took the gangster's hand which held the gun and crunched it against the wall behind; simultaneously, his right hand whipped to clutch the man's throat nerves, immediately paralysing him. The gun clattered to the floor and the hood's breath rattled as he gasped for air.

Gently and very slowly, Willard, his face coldly impassive, withdrew. The hood's neck burned with a deep pain and his hand was fractured and three fingers broken. For a split second, he thought of moving again, but Willard's eyes said not only *no* but that this time it would be more than his hand that would get broken.

'Now,' Willard said quietly, 'go and tell Gillamo that Qhe fulfilled his promise. All right? Then move!'

The hood backed awkwardly into the lift and Willard pressed the *down* button.

'I'll get you,' the man hissed as the doors slid shut, 'Oh boy will I get you.'

Willard stood watching the indicator above the door trace the lift's descent until it reached ground level, sadly shook his head and then carefully smoothed down his waistcoat and tie. It's funny, he thought to himself, how some guests never know how to leave gracefully.

SEVEN

While Marie and Purot slept, Qhe and Willard discussed everything that had happened and everything that might happen. As they talked, Qhe carefully polished the ivory bull which he had carved for his son. The gold had already been inlaid across its back and the three hundred rubies, saphires and amethysts had also already been inset into their small cavities. All that was needed now to complete his son's talisman was the second diamond, Gillamo's, for the right eye and a massive topaz to place in its forehead. Qhe knew that sooner or later he would acquire that diamond, but the only topaz that was suitable was in the British Crown Jewels in the Tower of London and . . .

'There are two things,' Willard was saying, 'that I want to check out. I want to have a look – a real look – at some of these people who are dying after being with the Prophets. I also want to take a look at how their money is being managed. It's struck me that there may be a silver lining to all this if it is Gillamo's crew that's looking after all the investments.'

'Yes?' Qhe looked up from the ivory bull. 'What sort of lining?'

'There's enough money, it seems to me, to make their criminal activities look like chickenfeed. It strikes me that they may not want to jeopardize it by anything illegal and that could mean, for instance, that they'll pull out of drugs – no more heroin.'

'Too good to be true,' Qhe answered. 'They're addicted to being criminals. If they weren't criminals, they'd curl up and waste away. I mean they couldn't wear sharkskin suits any more, could they? That's like a priest not being allowed to wear his cassock.'

'So?'

'I don't know,' Qhe replied. 'There's something that we

don't quite see.'

'I think we have the whole picture – it's just a matter of putting it in perspective. These trust funds and banks they're using, they're –'

'Good God!' Qhe exclaimed. 'Look at this – it's appeared from nowhere.'

He pointed at an enormous yellow topaz that lay on the table under the bull's belly. Qhe frowned, but at the same time felt a surging feeling of excitement rise in his stomach.

'Did,' he asked Willard hesitantly, 'did you put it here?'

Willard shook his head and immediately both men fell silent. The whole atmosphere in the room had changed; there was now something indefinably light and happy about it. There was a sensation of joy that brought tears to both men's eyes, but they swallowed hard and found themselves irresistibly smiling.

Without a knock, without warning, the door to the room opened.

'I hope that your child will appreciate our little present.'

The voice was deep with a strange ringing quality that held a hint of infinite humour and infinite seriousness. It belonged to a man in his fifties. He wore a suit of continental cut, but his bearing was that of a military aristocrat at ease. Qhe and Willard stood speechless. They looked into his deep grey eyes that sparkled compassionately, understandingly and humourously at them.

'Come,' the man said, 'let me kiss you both.'

He stepped forward and embraced first Willard and then Qhe. His grip was masculine and strong and yet it sent a thrill of absolute love through both men.

'How pleasant to see you both in the flesh,' he said warmly, 'but you must forgive me for arriving so unexpected.'

His last words held a hint of gentle mockery – not mockery of Qhe or Willard, but of himself.

'Let me look more closely at you.'

For a minute they stood there silently while he looked softly into their eyes. What he saw, what he was looking for, neither Qhe nor Willard could fathom and, indeed, it was unimportant to them. Merely to be in his presence was sufficient blessing.

'Yes, my little ones,' he continued, 'how much bigger you are getting!'

The three of them laughed until he raised his hand.

'I have little time to be with you, so listen carefully. That which you are about to fight is deeper and stronger than you think, but more important, there is the question of time. You understand my work and the laws within which I can help lay out the Plan. I cannot, therefore, interfere directly. No longer possessing karma, I cannot interfere with karma. I can only suggest, only provide a framework which a man's intuition can pick up – then it is for his mind to decide. We cannot interfere. Since the Great War of 1914 to 1945, I have been working to help the synthesis of nations. Much of it has been successful and the future will bring even greater evolution. However, there is always the question of money, of international finance, of cyclic and spiralling currency. Gradually, it is being worked out by the men of goodwill who work in government and finance. The problems are complex and take many years to resolve, but . . .'

He stopped as his eyes lit up and he looked to the door. The handle slowly turned and Qhe immediately moved to prevent whoever it was from entering, but the man's hand rose and the door opened. Almost sleep-walking, the journalist Marie de Baldeau entered the room.

'I was asleep, dreaming, but I felt something calling. I – I – I had to come.'

She looked questioningly around the room until her eyes focused on the guest and her lips broke into a gentle smile.

'I was right,' she said, not for one moment taking her eyes from him.

'Another little one,' the man said warmly. 'Come here.'

She walked slowly over to him and fell to her knees at his feet, but he immediately took her hand and raised her up. He then very gently kissed her hand and, for a few seconds, stood staring deep within her.

'It is time to focus your mind, Marie. This is no dream.

Now sit and listen.'

'Who are you?' she asked.

'You know already,' he replied. 'Ask no more. Let your questions float away. Let me continue my talk with your two brethren.'

She smiled again, but this time it was in full consciousness. Suddenly it seemed that she had come home, that she was where she truly belonged. Until that moment her life seemed completely meaningless and irrelevant. Her personality, the personality of Marie de Baldeau the photographer, seemed not to be hers. She was someone different who had been merely play-acting for the last twenty-five years. Who was she? she asked herself, but there came no answer to that question except that she had just begun her voyage of self-discovery.

'To return to my point,' the Adept continued. 'Gradually, the problems of world finance have been working out. There is the World Bank and the International Monetary Fund, and as you know international conferences have been held every year. Only recently have the men involved begun to envisage and comprehend the answers. It involves no great upheaval in organization, only in attitudes. It is this new attitude of common sense and global service that will break down the barriers of national egomania. Money is beginning to be seen as an international token for harmonious trade and relations and not as an isolated symbol of materialistic national prestige. A long lecture? But you must understand my work as I overshadow the thought-forms in which the financiers of the world operate. Later this year, there will be a conference in Kenya and at it decisions will be taken that will herald an era of true international co-operation. The thoughtform that surrounds it is perfect; the men involved are full of goodwill and tolerance. I paint no picture of an immediate paradise, but in the years and decades that follow, humanity will at last see itself properly as belonging to one global village in which everything material – and responsibility for everything material – is shared as in a family.'

He smiled at the three people in the room with him.

'It is a pity that I have no time to stay and chat,' he joked. 'Do not take the Prophets of the Prophet lightly. They work a devious evil on a plane too low for me to touch. Watch and deal with them very carefully. I can see a tentacle stretching out that may destroy the workings of our Plan. Deal with it at the very core. Know that it is filled with a greater and more negative power than you have yet seen. I can give you no more than this warning and I know that anyway you work your best. I am always watching. Know that I care.'

He stood abruptly and walked to the door.

'With love, with light and with power,' he whispered, then closed the door behind him.

'No,' Marie protested at his sudden departure.

She walked hurriedly across the room and opened the door. The man was gone. For a moment, her face held a look of total desolation, but then she smiled to herself and nodded.

'Phew,' she said.

'Phew indeed,' Qhe laughed. 'There's nothing to say, is there? Only that it is extremely rare and we are extremely lucky.'

'And you work for him?' she asked.

'Yes – and for his brothers,' Willard answered. 'Serve rather than work.'

'And may I serve too? Will you show me?'

'Ah, but you will show yourself – every man shows himself.'

'There's so much . . .'

Her words trailed off interrupted by the ringing of Qhe's private phone. He answered it immediately and switched on the extension speaker so that Willard could listen.

'Hello, Qhe? It's Sir Gerald here. How are you?'

'I'm well and you?'

'Fine, fine,' answered Sir Gerald Pollinger, Permanent Under-Secretary at the Ministry of Defence in London. 'And Willard?'

'He's well and listening at the moment. What is it, Gerald?'

'Damned strange, Qhe, most peculiar. I've known about this for a few days now, but just had a sudden flash that I had to tell you. About a minute ago, someone seemed to nudge the back of my mind – does that make sense?'

'Absolutely,' Qhe replied. 'That *someone* just did more than nudge the back of our minds. What do you have?'

'Look, it's like this. Some stock market boys along with some Treasury investigators are doing a full-scale investigation of a mammoth multi-national conglomerate – Trusts International Incorporated. They've money in everything, but especially in property, leisure and North Sea oil. However, there's something about the way that they move their capital and actually get hold of their finances that doesn't quite ring true. Four days ago the Governor of the Bank of England received a letter saying that if the investigation wasn't called off then enough sterling would suddenly be slid onto the open market to cause a twenty-five per cent devaluation. Believe me, the pound couldn't stand it.'

'And you believe the threat?' Willard asked.

'No choice, old boy. The note also said that there'd be a hint of what was to come and within twenty-four hours enough sterling was sold to send the pound rocking from here to Zurich and back to Hong Kong. Of course, that could be coincidence. That's the way they want to treat it, but ... Does all this mean anything to you?'

'It means enough,' Qhe answered. 'Have there been similar threats in any other capitals?'

'The Treasury doesn't dare ask. The value of money, you understand, is based on confidence. Any rumour at the moment could set everything shaking.'

'Have you tried to find out yourself?' Willard asked.

'I will now – gently of course. Is there anything else I can do for you? I must say I'm pretty damned relieved you know something about all this.'

'No,' Qhe replied. 'Just see if it's happening anywhere else – and thanks for calling.'

'Don't thank me,' Sir Gerald joked back.

The telephone clicked. Marie lit a cigarette and looked quizzically at Qhe then Willard.

'Phew,' she whistled. 'You know, this should be really blowing my mind, but there's something so ... so normal about it all, about the way you are. Magicians! Sorcerers! Wizards! It should seem crazy. Phone calls from people like that – and, trust me, I won't mention it to anyone. And you know the craziest thing?'

Both Qhe and Willard shook their heads.

'The craziest thing is that you should be weird – and you're not! More than that, it's the most commonsensical and sophisticated scene I've ever been in. Really. And...'

She looked away shyly.

'You feel,' Willard finished her sentence for her, 'that you're one of us.'

She nodded, lowered her gaze and then looked hesitantly up at the two men. She nodded again.

'And now?' she asked.

'I must call some of my men over to help us,' Qhe answered. 'And as you now believe in magic, this won't surprise you. Just a bit of silence.'

He sat crosslegged on the floor and began to breathe very gently and rhythmically. Within a minute his body and mind were calm, and then he raised his consciousness. He willed it upwards until there was not a single emotional distraction and then higher so that there were no stray thoughts, and then higher still until it floated in the realm of pure intuitive thought.

From that point in an ocean of peace, he could scan the globe with his mind like a psychic radar disc. He tuned into his home high in the Himalayan mountains, into a white stone tower that stood over a white palace built in the shape of a seven-pointed star. Then he tensed his body and sent his message.

EIGHT

The Pashmani priest, ninety-seven years old and with a few strands of silvery white hair falling down his back from his almost totally bald head, had been sitting in the tower for over seven hours. He was nearing the end of his watch when the call came through from his king. He had held his mind completely clear for those seven hours and there was not the slightest doubt in him about the message or its sender. He recognized the note, the vibration of Qhe, as clearly as if they were only a few feet apart.

He did not move immediately, but held still for another fifteen minutes to make absolutely certain that what he had received still rang true. He then rang a small silver gong and his replacement, a young priest, barely in his twenties, came to take his place. The old man said nothing, but slowly descended the spiral staircase down into a side courtyard of the palace.

As he walked across the yard, he gently clapped his hands in time with the small group of white-robed royal musicians who sat playing wood-flutes and tiny finger cymbals. He walked down a long corridor, its walls engraved with brilliant mosaics symbolically depicting the course of our galaxy through the cosmos, and finally he entered a chamber where two other priests stood talking.

The appearance of the old man was enough for one of them to leave the room immediately. Within seconds, the bellowing sound of a mammoth, curved elephant-tusk horn could he heard echoing through the palace. But its noise carried beyond the royal home, across the lake at the centre of which it stood, and over the capital city of Gensang. The robed peasants, merchantmen, priests and priestesses, the women and all the children heard the elephant-tusk call and the whole city fell silent as every single inhabitant stopped to say a silent prayer. They prayed for the safety of their king, for the harmony of the world and for the warriors who would soon go to help Qhe.

From four corners of the city, four more horns were sounded, their notes reverberating across the emerald green countryside. Every quarter mile, the call was taken up so that the message could be carried all over the Kingdom of Pashman. Legend told that when these horns were blown even the giant peaks of the Himalayas, in which stood the two hundred mile long sloping valley that was Pashman, took notice and sent out a vibration for peace across the planet.

And in the country, seventy young men whose life-path was to make war alongside their King-Priest, dropped their pens or holy books or ploughs and began to make for the palace.

Within the palace itself, eighty beautiful women, Qhe's secular wives, filed slowly and with immense dignity into a side temple. They seemed to glide along the marble floor as they took their positions to form the pattern of the seven-pointed star. All in place, they simultaneously lowered themselves crosslegged to the floor. Except for short breaks these eighty women would stay like this for as long as was needed, even to their deaths – their devotion and loving care would send out a bubble of gentle rose-coloured light to protect their king and husband.

In yet another temple in the palace, other priests prepared for their rituals and worship, not so much for Qhe's protection but to send waves of light through the minds of evil men. Elsewhere, the court astrologers carefully began studying the charts of Qhe, of Willard, of humanity and of the planet as a whole. In this manner they could see when crisis points might occur and over those times the priests would intensify their ceremonial. Another group of priests monitored the world's radio stations to pick up special area's of conflict where they might send their energies.

Within two hours, the Palace had settled into the rhythm of its planetary work and it was backed up by the work in all the other temples of Pashman. The warriors themselves now began to arrive. They were all dressed in loose-hanging violet slacks and tops similar to western pyjamas and each one had a deadly clear look in his eyes. They were all under thirty, slim and lithely built. Deadly expert in all forms of combat, they each carried only one weapon, the Pashmani knife with its four-inch long handle carved from elephant-tusk and its five-inch steel blade no thicker than a knitting needle but with three cutting edges, each razor sharp. From birth these men had also been rigidly trained in the other Pashmani disciplines – the yogas of body, of mind, of worship and of love. To be their friend or brother was to feel protection and warmth, and they always assumed that every man was their brother – until shown otherwise. For a man who was their enemy, however, they were inutterably dangerous. They owed their love and protection to any man, but their allegiance was solely to Qhe.

They spent an hour in the palace, praying and preparing, before setting forth for the mountains to the north of Gen-sang. They took a path that led them alongside one of the streams, created by the melting snows, and through a forty acre park devoted solely to flowers, flowering shrubs and trees. Where the stream formed into pools, naked children played adding their own high-spirited gurgles to the sound of the water. They waved enthusiastically to the warriors who laughed and waved back and performed small acrobatic tricks to entertain their younger friends. The air was filled with the scent of lilac, wild rose and an army of other radiating blossoms. In the trees and bushes sat multi-coloured birds of paradise, temporarily silent as the men walked past them.

The warriors reached a huge cliff and began to mount the steps carved into its side. They climbed over five hundred feet until the steps reached a tunnel that led through the mountain. Before entering it, they stopped for a few seconds to turn and take one last look back down the valley. The view was spectacular across the flower garden with its silver sparkling streams and then the city of Gen-sang with its white towers and dome and, to the city's side, the Royal Palace. Beyond all that, they could see almost a hundred miles down the fifty mile wide sloping valley of

Pashman with the gleaming snow-capped peaks on either side. Each of the warriors smiled gently to himself before turning to enter the tunnel.

The walls of the rough-hewn passageway shone and glittered with thousands of tiny gems for the tunnel passed through the peak known as the Mountain of Infinite Eyes. Pashmani lore told that if any man were to remove a single of these precious stones for personal gain, then the mountain – and the rest of the world with it – would collapse. Not one stone had ever been touched.

The tunnel opened on to a plateau that had been carved out of the mountain side. Unlike Pashman which belonged to eternity, this shelf was owned by the twentieth century. There was the smell of oil and petrol, and the deafening noise of jet engines. This plateau had been constructed like the deck of an aircraft carrier and on it the Pashmani Royal Jet Two was ready for take-off.

NINE

The Arab security men guarding the private clinic in the countryside near Geneva did not stop Willard as he casually walked up the steps to its entrance. In his pinstripe suit with a red carnation in his lapel, he looked too like a visiting English surgeon to raise any suspicions. Once inside the clinic, he asked the nurse at reception for her registry book and without a second's hesitation she handed it over.

Skimming through it, he quickly noted the room numbers of the patients whom he wished to visit, then made his way to their rooms which were all situated on one corridor on the second floor. Greeting the sister-in-charge, he informed her that he was not to be disturbed. She was about to ask for his authority, but he spoke before she had a chance:

'The Ministry sent me,' he told her. 'Now, please, no interruptions. I shan't be long.'

For some strange reason she found herself about to curtsy and only just managed to stop herself.

'Yes doctor, of course,' she stuttered.

He walked briskly to one of the rooms and entered. The young man from Saudi Arabia was in his early thirties and his normally dark complexion was horribly pale.

'Salam alaikum,' Willard greeted him in Arabic. 'How are you?'

The man tried to raise his head, but his neck muscles just did not have the power to lift it.

'I am as God wills it,' he finally answered.

'Of course, of course.'

Willard walked over and looked at the charts hanging on the end of the man's bed. Blood pressure down. Heart beat down. Temperature down. Everything was normal except that the man was just wasting away. There was no virus in his body, no glandular changes and no kind of injury. He looked carefully at the man's face. The expression was totally bland. There was a complete acceptance of what was happening to him.

'Well now, do you want to tell me how it happened?'

For the first time, the man reacted. His lips thinned and he looked agressively up at Willard.

'You will tell me nothing?' Willard asked gently.

The man nodded and Willard nodded back in sympathy.

'I am, you know,' Willard said, 'in sympathy with the Prophets of the Prophet.'

'Yes, yes, they work the will of Allah. Only the will of Allah. Always the will of Allah.'

'Tell me then.'

The man smiled and shook his head.

'For the present it is secret, but the future is glorious.'

'Allah's future is always glorious,' Willard agreed.

'Yes, yes,' the man repeated, as a look of enraptured bliss crossed his face.

'It was worth it then?'

'Unbeliever, unbeliever,' the man sing-songed back at him. 'To see the face of Allah's Prophet – anything is worth it. To Him, I gave myself. If now I am taken ... Allah's will, always Allah's will and that of His Prophet.'

'His Prophet?' Willard queried.

'Ah,' The man sighed blissfully, but would say no more.

Had he wished to speak, he no longer had any strength. His energies were exhausted. Willard stood looking down at the limp body of the demented man. What, he asked himself, what on earth was the physiological cause for this man's illness and imminent death? For some reason, there was no energy, no energy at all, flowing into him.

He left the room and entered the next one, but here the man was on the verge of death. Again, however, his face held no look of remorse or sadness. The third room, was occupied by a grey-haired Iraqi, who lay in bed incoherently mumbling passages from the Koran. In the fourth room, the patient was able to talk to Willard.

His message and words were exactly those of the first man. It was all Allah's will. Everything had been worth it. Then just a single mention of the Prophet before he refused to speak further. Willard gained no further information from the other patients. It was absolutely impossible to probe these dying men any deeper. What they wanted to tell him, what they could tell him, they had. They believed that it was Allah's will, that everything was as it should be, that everything was perfect. The younger generation, Willard thought, had a good phrase for this: blissed out. These men had been totally blissed out of their minds – and, shortly, out of their bodies. They had seen the face of the Prophet and that had made everything worthwhile. The Prophet?

As he walked out of the clinic, Willard almost slapped his own face in anger. The Prophet. Just *one* Prophet. Who the hell . . .?

As he got into his hired car the sun reflected off something shiny a few hundred feet away. Adjusting the car mirror, he looked carefully behind him and watched as two men in shark-skin suits and dark glasses climbed into their American limousine. Willard frowned and a shiver ran down his spine. He was in no mood for more bloody nonsense. The vegetable-like quality of the men in the clinic had annoyed him – he did not like the way in which they had been interfered with. He did not bother to consider whether the two men in the car were simply tailing him or had other more deadly instructions: he just did not feel like continually peering over his shoulder.

He took his umbrella from the back seat and began to stroll casually down the road as if taking his morning walk in St James's Park. He neared the car and could feel the gangsters' confusion as their target approached. It was now, only fifty feet away, that Willard knew for certain what their orders had been – it was the infallible instinct of a man who had experienced, and lived through, too many dangerous and threatening situations.

The road was silent, the perfect place for an unobserved murder, but not mine, Willard thought. He crossed it to walk by the grass on the opposite side to the car. He stopped and knelt to study a couple of wild flowers, apparently oblivious of the car and its occupants. He held the flowers carefully in his cupped hand, smelled their sweet fragrance then moved forward. It was only when he was directly opposite the car that he stopped and absent-mindedly looked into it.

The two men were cold-blooded professionals and their hands moved smoothly to their shoulder holsters. They had not planned it this way, but the opportunity was too good to miss. They had been told the Englishman was dangerous, but right now he looked like the easiest hit in the world. The boys back in New York would not believe it when they were told how their mark had just simply walked up to them like a lamb to the slaughter.

'Excuse me, gentlemen,' Willard shouted across the road.

In answer, the man in the driver's seat slowly wound down his window.

'I'm sorry to disturb you,' Willard continued, 'but I was –'

'– No disturbance,' the man replied as he pulled out his revolver.

Willard shut up at the sight of the weapon and his face assumed a look of panicked surprise. His mouth twisted and his eyes screwed up.

'You c-can't,' he stuttered.

'Watch us,' the man replied as his finger squeezed the trigger.

Willard's eyes had only been narrowed so that he could watch the man's hand more carefully. As the gun fired, he hurled himself down and forward, somersaulting across the road. Coming up, he leaped forward holding his umbrella like a rapier. With his whole weight behind it, its point smashed into the man's skull before a second shot could be fired, instantly killing him. The force of the blow was so great that he crashed across the seat cracking his partner's head against the inside of the car.

Willard straightened his tie not even bothering to look into the car. He found the whole affair distasteful and he knew that if he stopped even for a second to meditate on what had just happened, he would want to fall on his knees to weep and to pray. Instead, his back held straight and his chin firmly forward, he walked back to his own car. He wanted to work magic – not death.

'From now on,' Qhe hissed at Gillamo, 'you will show some respect. I've played your petty game for long enough. I've had enough of mincing around in this stinking bourgeois hole of yours. I've had enough of being polite. I tried to do all this pleasantly, but your childish fantasies have gone too far.'

Gillamo opened his mouth to try and speak, but Qhe's furious blazing eyes prevented him.

'Your insult to me with that gorilla I was prepared to ignore, but your clumsy attempt on Willard went too far. Do you understand that to me you're no more than a slug I would not even deign to crush with my own heel? You're the worst kind of mindless vermin that exists. You're not worth a skunk's fart. And you even dare to think that you're heavy! Heavy? You're as lightweight as a flea on the neck of a dead dog. And then you talk about your all-powerful family! Power? You don't know the difference between power and running a spinsters' knitting circle. Your family is like a pack of rats. Your family stinks. You make me sick.'

Gillamo was sweating and angry beyond belief. No one in the world could talk to a Don like this. No one! There was no longer time even to think about talking to this Qhe – he had to be wiped out now. Gillamo walked across to the bar.

'You've gone too far,' he spat.

'Go on,' Qhe taunted, 'press your button and see what happens.'

Gillamo's mind flashed with momentary panic as he pressed the emergency button that would call in his men. Having pressed it, he looked at Qhe and snorted.

'I have thirty men on this estate. Any one of them would die for me, for the family. Anyone of them, Qhe, would kill you just for one of those words that you have spoken!'

'Of course,' Qhe answered gently, 'but look out of the window.'

Gillamo smiled smugly, sneered and then turned. The

swimming pool which had shortly before contained three bikinied starlets was empty. Nor was there any of his men lounging beside it.

'So what?' Gillamo asked.

'Where are your men?' Qhe replied. 'Isn't it time that you pressed your little button again?'

'They'll have heard it.'

Immediately he said this, the door opened and one of Qhe's warriors, in his violet fighting tunic, entered. He bowed gracefully to both men.

'Everything is quiet, Your Majesty,' he said and then immediately withdrew.

'Don Gillamo,' Qhe said gently, 'believe me, I don't want to kill you. I just want your co-operation.'

'You win this battle,' Gillamo shouted, 'but you don't win the war!'

Qhe sighed and shook his head.

'Just give me a slice of the action, Gillamo. You know that I could blow this whole scene for you. What do you think the other Dons would want – me to blow it, or me to have a slice? To lose a percentage or to have a war with me – whoever wins? Accept gracefully.'

Gillamo grunted and shook his head.

'I'd rather die,' he spat.

'But it could be far, far worse for you, brother,' Qhe answered sinisterly. 'Haven't you noticed anything weird since you became involved with the Prophets. Haven't you noticed that things are ... well ... spooky? Haven't you noticed strange atmospheres? A constant feeling that something's always behind your back?'

Gillamo laughed at this.

'You know you're messing with religion?'

These last words of Qhe were spoken with a vehemence and sincerity that cut deep into Gillamo. The last person to use such a tone with him had been the priest in Sicily.

'You're shoving morality down my throat?'

'Morality? No,' Qhe answered. 'Truth? Yes. Are you moving so fast and so greedily that you don't see what you're involved in? Haven't you felt it? You don't mix with men like that without picking up some of their energies.'

'You're crazy.'

'Crazy? Stop for a second and feel.'

As he stopped speaking, he willed Gillamo to feel the sudden silence. The house was deadly quiet. For two minutes they stood there, saying nothing, all the time Qhe willing the atmosphere to thicken and intensify.

'Don't you feel it?' he asked Gillamo in the most friendly, fraternal tone. 'It's like a web that covers everything. Eyes everywhere. Did you never notice that those three men – the Prophets – were more than just crazy or greedy? Couldn't you see it in them?'

'This is bullshit,' Gillamo replied, but he found himself whispering the words empty of any conviction.

Qhe was right. The atmosphere did feel damned strange, like you could cut it with a knife. Sure it was spooky.

'Possession,' Qhe continued. 'There are things all around that could possess you. Can you imagine what would happen if you tried to disengage from the Prophets? There'd be no guns, would there, but you'd be hounded for the rest of your life, frightened to sleep, worse than the peasants on your island.'

Gillamo's body went cold and he felt the hair on the back of his neck beginning to tremble. Somewhere at the back of his mind a voice told him Qhe was fooling, but when he looked up at his face, he was greeted by a pair of penetrating eyes that insisted that all this was the truth.

'When you make a racket out of religion,' Qhe said, 'you know . . .' He nodded meaningfully.

'You,' Gillamo still whispered, 'you believe in this crap?'

Qhe's eyes darted as if he had suddenly seen something in the corner of the room and Gillamo shuddered. Qhe slowly looked round the room, his face watchful and anxious.

'You should just know the whole situation. You know what I mean, Gillamo?'

The Don breathed in deeply and sighed. He needed a drink. He needed a cigarette. Maybe he even needed retirement.

'Do you think,' Qhe asked, 'that my men could walk all over yours if you weren't fighting something else at the same time?'

Gillamo winced. For a few minutes he had totally forgotten that not only was he vulnerable to these 'energies' he was also vulnerable to Qhe. Suddenly, he was a very lonely man.

'In my country,' Qhe confided, 'we know how to protect ourselves. Now do you want to give me a slice? It seems the easiest alternative for you – the best way of making business.'

Before waiting for Gillamo's answer, he clapped his hands. Within a few seconds there was the sound of giggling and splashing. Gillamo spun round to look out of the window. The pool again contained his starlets, but on either side of it, looking calmly at the house, were a half dozen Pashmani warriors. They nodded to Gillamo as if to say that everything was in perfect order.

'It's a deal then, isn't it?' Qhe asked.

Gillamo nodded. By now he was prepared to agree to anything and he led Qhe through to his office to show him all the relevant papers.

TEN

Qhe sat crosslegged before the altar in the small five-walled temple at the top of the International Gems Building. His energies were intensely focused around his forehead and he was carefully scanning around the room.

'It seems secure to me,' he said.

'It is, dear brother, it is,' Willard agreed. 'The meeting is due to begin very soon, so . . . so, bon voyage.'

'You too,' Qhe smiled. 'I'm certain you'll do only too well at the Conference of the Dons.'

Willard also smiled.

'We shall see,' he answered and then, first crossing himself, withdrew from the temple.

Qhe now began to breathe very slowly and rhythmically. He gently ensured that every single muscle of his body was totally relaxed and, when this was the case, he changed the pace of his breathing. He pulled air in for a count of eight, held it for a further count of eight, exhaled over eight and then waited again for a count of eight before recommencing the cycle. As he did this, he visualized the whole room around him glittering with a silver sheen and each inhalation sucked this shining energy into his body. Holding his breath he visualized his body absorbing the energy and on the out-breath he imagined it gradually filling his feet and legs. Over a period of five minutes, he poured this energy into himself until every fibre of his physical being was saturated with it.

He now allowed his breathing to break the eight-eight-eight-eight pattern and it immediately fell into a gentle rhythm of its own. It was so shallow that to an onlooker it would have been barely noticeable, as if he was sleeping, but his mind was crystal clear. From this point of calm, he mentally forced more energy into his body and at the same time dilated and expanded his stomach to massage his solar plexus. Almost immediately he felt his legs begin to stiffen and then inch by inch his whole body became rigid as if paralysed or in a hypnotic trance.

Everything perfectly in order, he willed his consciousness, centred as it was in his forehead, towards the back of his head and then began to raise it. He heard a distant and extremely high-pitched whistling noise, he felt intense pressure on the top of his skull and then, with the noise of a pea popping out of its pod, he was free of his physical body.

Now in his astral body, he hovered a few feet above his inert physical frame and looked carefully around him. As always, he was momentarily awed by the wonder and brilliance of the colours on the astral and mental planes. The dense matter of his body and of the building was now opaque. What seemed a thousand times more real were the beautiful swirling colours within the temple, the colours that existed in every place of worship. Here also could be seen the small elementals, the younger brothers of what westerners call Angels, whose purpose was to help a human being's worship and devotion. Qhe smiled at seeing them and they, in magnetic sympathy, returned his smile. He looked with satisfaction at the gleaming astral crosses and pentagrams that stood around his body as protection so that while he was gone nothing else could enter his empty dwelling.

In this exteriorised state, his astral body would move at the speed of which he allowed himself to think. As a youth being trained by the Pashmani magician-priests it had taken him many months to learn to control his mind when out of his body. Everything had been so wonderful that his mind had raced uncontrollably, taking him here, there and everywhere like an elfin flash of lightning. Now, years later, he was still always tempted just to allow his mind to roam and to take his body where fancy willed it. Today, however, there was work to be done.

He floated himself up and out of the building. Not focusing properly, the city of Marseilles looked like a swarming volcano of murky colours, the unmistakeable aura of any large materialistic metropolis. In stark contrast lay the gleaming Mediterranean Sea, the sparkling sky and the huge glowing orb of the sun – all these in colours that defy human description.

Qhe turned his mind to Grenobles and faster than the speed of light found himself above it. The chateau was to the north in the mountains and he turned in that direction, letting his mind probe outwards for the correct vibration. Within seconds he had tuned in to its sinister magnetism and, within a split second, was floating a few hundred feet above it. His astral body immediately shivered at the negative charge of electricity surrounding the old French building. If definitive proof had ever been needed of the Prophets' evil, it was provided here.

On the astral plane, the whole area was permeated with a grey-green colour with flashes of deepest purple and flaming red. Qhe inwardly winced at the terrible vision and wondered whether the Prophets had put up any special protection. He now moved very carefully, allowing himself to absorb and feel every nuance and hint of this horrible texture. Having moved three times around the chateau, he had seen and felt nothing, but he could not believe that there were no astral guards. It was no use waiting for them to find him and he vibrated out a call to attract anything malicious that might be in the area.

Instantaneously he felt something behind him, threatening and extremely dangerous, but he did not turn to confront it. Like a matador turning his back on the enraged bull, Qhe held himself calmly while intensely aware of the aggressive fiend. *Closer, come closer*, he vibrated his message out to it. The texture of the light around him began to change and, again, he felt himself trembling. In total concentration, his mind focused on the fact that he was invulnerable just as long as he was unafraid, he still did not turn.

He could now sense the fiend taunting and threatening him. *Closer, come closer*, Qhe called out. *I know you, I do not fear you – I am of such strength that I may absorb you.* At this, the fiend began immediately to back away, but Qhe willed it to stay close. *I can and I may absorb you,* Qhe repeated. *In the name of Light and Love do I have power and dominion over you.* The blob of malevolent energy began to thrash and twist to escape this traveller of light, but Qhe still held it close.

With all his strength and confidence, Qhe extended a web of energy from himself to embrace and hold the beast who was now magnetically bellowing and roaring to escape. *Be calm*, Qhe ordered. *Be instantly calm!* Like an angry sea subsiding after a storm, the demon became quiet. It had no mind, but worked instinctively by vibration and attraction. In the same way that opposite poles of a magnet are drawn together, so this astral creature was drawn to anything that held white light to attack and frighten it off. Caught by Qhe, unable to threaten this man, the creature only desired release.

Qhe turned to look at it. He surveyed it coolly and impassively. It was formed in the shape of a terrifying gothic monster, the murky form of a gigantic demon with glowing red eyes and flabby, draping, moulding skin. Qhe held the demon immobile with his fixed look, then shot a vibration of high frequency aggression against it. The demon shuddered and thrashed frantically to escape, but Qhe still held it close. *Leave me alone*, Qhe told it, *leave me alone*.

Now he released it and the demon sped like a flash of lightning to a safe distance. Nothing could make him approach this man again, nothing.

Qhe turned his attention back to the chateau and his attention was irresistibly drawn to the hall containing the hundred people who were waiting eagerly to see the Prophets. Every emotion and thought has a different colour on the astral and mental planes – they are colours, however, that bear little relation to the colours that we know on our materialistic plane of existence. They are colours that exist in a spectrum far beyond our normal vision, colours that are hinted at by modern scientific knowledge of infra-red and ultra-violet.

Qhe's years of training with the magician-priests of Pashman had well-educated him in recognizing the meaning of the different colour tones and hues. Looking at the crowd of one hundred people, his immediate feeling was one of sympathy at their innocent devotion and expectancy. They had come here because a network of subtle spiritual propaganda promised them eternal answers to infinite problems and a blessing that would transcend all wordly problems. The majority of them were Muslims, steeped from childhood in the religious, prophetic poetry of the Koran, poetry that promised them Heaven if they followed the way – Islam – of Allah and his Prophet Mohammed.

In the propaganda and lectures that they had heard, they had all caught a hint of an imminent and glorious happening. Their brethren who had been to the Chateau before them had promised miracles, the like of which no man had seen for over a thousand years and rumours were rife that told of a special internal group of disciples that had actually seen ... seen what? They did not know, but they did know that brothers and friends who had entered this special group had experienced a vision of such wonder and glory that afterwards they only desired – and received – death. What bliss! What promises! What paradise!

Their one-pointed expectancy and devotion shone through their astral auras. There were nine men, however, who, although they play-acted equal expectancy and religious fervour, were calm and knowing. These were nine of the Pashmani warriors.

Qhe turned his attention to the rest of the chateau and focused in on the Prophets' henchmen. There were twenty of them and they were a strange bunch of psychic hooligans. They had all originally come from Gillamo's contacts, but had been with the Prophets for so long now that their whole mental and emotional make-up had changed. The hard look of a street hoodlum had been changed for a macabre holier-than-thou expression: the sort of expression that said *love God or I'll do you.* Their underworld psychopathy was now strengthened by religious fervour and demented belief.

The trio of ungodly imposters who claimed to be Prophets were currently preparing themselves for their meeting with their disciples. Qhe shuddered at his first glimpse of them for their auras were filthy beyond belief. Not a single colour indicating the slightest trace of anything emotionally or mentally good and evolutionary existed around them. More than that, however, they were filled with great power, the power that belonged to the single-minded fanatic of involutionary magic.

The three men were silent as they donned their robes and prepared themselves for their disciples. They readied themselves for their performance with disciplined professionalism. Their lives were geared to events such as this when they could display their almighty power and be gratified by their hypnotic control over their audience. In this way, they also served their master and his ends.

They also claimed to be immortal, but from Qhe's astral viewpoint it was only too obvious how human they were, unable to resist the temptation that brought them their bizarre force. He was on the point of probing more deeply into them when they began to move towards the main hall. It was as they walked that he saw the bond of energies that held them together as a triangle of power, but he had no time to study it as they entered.

Immediately he could see the disciples' waves of nervous flowing devotion and at the same time the aura of triangular power expanded to fill the hall. When one of the Prophets spoke, a line of light shot out from him and entered the aura of one of the onlookers. Every sentence uttered carried with it this thread of energy until after a few minutes every person in the hall was held in a gossamer web of energy. The Prophets played with their audience like maestros conducting a symphony orchestra, plucking every astral chord until the audience reached a fever pitch of expectation.

And then came the levitation. The triangular force of energies was focused solely into the Persian and Qhe watched as the very substance of his material body seemed to change its quality. Its electric vibrations were being reversed so that the magnetic hold of the Earth's gravity no longer affected it. This indeed was the work of a master magician and it was this train of thought that suddenly raised a question mark in Qhe's mind. These three men were initiates of certain sorcerous secrets, but they were not master magicians. This power of reversing the electric charge in a human body was not theirs. It came from elsewhere.

ELEVEN

From a mile above the chateau, the connecting thread of energy was unmistakable. Qhe had only not noticed it before because he had been too close, but at this height it could be seen clearly as a man-made electricity pylon disappearing into the distance towards the south-west.

He began to follow it and within seconds had passed Marseilles and was shooting over the Mediterranean. His course took him down the coast of Spain and then past the Balearic Islands. A few seconds more and he was approaching the northern coastline of Morocco and then crossing the three moutain ranges of the Rif, the Middle Atlas and the High Atlas. As he passed over the highest mountain in North Africa, Mount Toupkal, the view before him changed spectacularly. The landscape ahead glowed like burning gold for as far as he could see. The shimmer of an ocean of heatwaves rolled back and forth across the vast expanse of the Sahara Desert.

Only occasionally were there tiny pockets of life and civilization, and these oases stood out like glimmering tiny green jewels lost in the sea of brilliant yellow. He had never before travelled across this area and he was astounded by its primitive beauty, even stopping for a few minutes to gaze in awe at the landscape below. Clever, clever God, he said to himself, grand artist of the cosmos, oh One Divine. He was filled for a moment with that wondrous sense of mystic unity in which everything became a glorious void and he just a part of that void.

He psychically shook his head to bring himself back to more mundane reality and continued his flight following the path of energy. It took him across the border of Algeria and into the Republic of Mali, where, thousands of miles from anywhere, he reached his destination. He could see the area from two hundred miles so great was its aura. In the shape of a perfect cube – the cube symbolic of dense matter – its astral form was at least half a mile high and half a mile wide. Its colour was grey streaked with purple and it was the most sinister thing that Qhe had ever seen. It slowly throbbed and vibrated out a magnetism of sucking materialism and greed, of energy that could reverse the whole process of divine and natural evolution.

Cautiously steeling himself against it, Qhe approached. To the side of this astral cube was a small airstrip, but there were no aircraft upon it and it was of little interest. Qhe increased his own altitude and now approached to about five miles distance to peer intensely into the grey and purple mist. It took him a little time to focus on the ground at the centre of the area for it was difficult to make out exactly what there was there. Gradually it came into vision.

An enormous hollow had been excavated out of the ground, again in the shape of a perfect cube, one hundred yards square. At its centre stood a gleaming black cube, twenty yards square. It was from this sinister central core that the pulsating evil energy was emanating and, Qhe wondered, who knew what was beneath this deep in the earth.

He moved even closer to try to scan within the cube. A mile away from the grey astral aura the pressure on his body was immense and made his movement almost impossible. It was as if he was trying to run through treacle and, at the same time, a severe electric charge was passing through him. Half a mile from it, he decided that he had no choice but to withdraw and properly prepare himself. It was as he began to float away that he saw a strange new movement on the surface of the astral cube.

For an area of about thirty square yards, pressure was building up on the surface of the cube and making it bubble and undulate. Fascinated, Qhe stopped to watch this bizarre phenomenon which reminded him of the bubbling of volcanic lava. It seemed as if part of the matter of the astral cube was trying to free itself, but the surface tension was too great for it to break away. At regular pulsating intervals, the bubble pushed further and further out from the surface of the cube until finally it covered two thirds of its surface.

Suddenly it began to change shape, thinning out and extending into the sky like an ever-stretching tentacle. Qhe's fascination turned into total apprehension as this macabre feeler moved directly towards him. Without hesitating a second, Qhe began to move away but the treacly texture of the atmosphere had thickened threefold. It was now a matter of pure will power to move through it, as he painfully pushed himself away from the tentacle which was moving smoothly and effortlessly towards him.

For the first time in years, Qhe felt the creeping sensation of claustrophobic panic. *Calm*, he told himself, *calm*. If he could just orientate his mindpower correctly then he could be gone like an arrow from a bow. He needed to focus himself so dynamically that he could just blast himself away and out of the area. Even thinking this, he watched the grey astral feeler coming even closer. *Be calm*, he told himself again, but he seemed to hear his own thought as an echo from someone else. *Who said that*? he asked himself. *Who said that? I did. Who? Me.* He was completely disorientated. One part of his mind was clear, but the rest of him was vibrating horribly from the threat.

Again he tried to move, but the atmosphere now seemed as thick as mud and his whole body thrilled as if he had been placed in a two hundred and forty volt electric circuit. He was immobile and rigid, held like a rat in a trap, as the tentacle reached only a hundred yards away. His body began to shiver in that uncontrollable feeling of panic at his impending destruction. His mind stopped working coolly and his reactions and feelings were instinctive – the instinct of a Pashmani warrior king. If he were to be destroyed it would be with thundering glory. He would turn all the throbbing energy of panic to a different use.

He held his astral hands forward and imagined them to be holding an enormous gleaming double-handed golden sword. Qhe's whole force now focused itself into a stance of complete aggression. His would be no gentle destruction. He looked to the tentacle and psychically screamed at it to come closer quicker. *I am a warrior of light*! he screamed. *I fight for glory. No sickening sludge of evil will take me lightly. I fight as an Angel with a flaming sword of golden truth.*

The tentacle groped closer and Qhe, holding out his sword, began to spin his body until he was just a swirling vortex of silver and gold light. Then, when the malicious feeler was only a few feet away, with a glorious cry of love for light, Qhe hurled himself forward to attack.

There were blinding flashes of different coloured light and the whole world seemed to shake and thunder at the battle. He felt himself held and twisted in the air, but still he spun and wielded his sword. He convulsed and shook. He would not allow himself to be held by this manacle of evil. He would destroy it. He would destroy everything evil. Nothing bad would remain. All grey and black would disappear. He was God's avenger. He alone would balance the energies of the planet. He alone would protect and save the light of the world. He felt the macabre energy clamping down on him even stronger and correspondingly he increased his wild efforts. He was a thunderbolt. a godling of fire, at battle with primeval forces.

Second by second the grey energy took a greater hold on him. Second by second he felt himself being held closer and squeezed down into nothingness. *No!* he screamed. *Never!* With one last mighty thunderous effort, he thrashed to free himself and destroy the evil. There was a resounding cracking sound and, in a split second, everything changed.

For only a moment but it seemed like an eternity, there was no sound, no light, no colour, no feeling, no sensation, no texture. He was in limbo, in a vacuum in which he himself was vacuum. Nothingness.

Then there was a light whistling noise like a cannon shell passing overhead and he crashed down to earth.

In the small temple at the top of the building in Marseilles, Qhe's physical body was thrown violently across the room to crash against the door. It convulsed twice, then twitched and then was still. Thirty seconds later, his eyes slowly and cautiously opened. He lifted his head and looked around. His eyes were glazed and bweildered. He could not fully believe where he was.

With extreme care, he lifted his bruised body up from the temple floor. Once on his feet, he gingerly flexed his muscles. Nothing was broken. Everything was still in one piece.

Gradually a small smile began to break across his lips. A few seconds later it cracked into a broad grin.

'What a pantomime!' he said aloud to himself and laughed. 'Back in my body, eh? Home sweet home.'

Then, as he dropped to his knees in front of the altar to give thanks, the door to the temple opened and three of his warriors entered. Their expressions were concerned and anxious.

'We're sorry,' one of them apologised, 'but suddenly we felt that something was . . .'

Qhe raised his hand to stop the man continuing and turned round to look at his three Pashmani brothers.

'There was,' he said, grateful for their love and concern. 'There was indeed, but come kneel with me for a while.'

The three warriors moved gracefully across the temple and knelt beside their king. Qhe now clapped his hands eleven times in a particular rhythm and together the men began to chant a prayer of worship.

TWELVE

'No, that's all right,' Qhe told his men. 'A quarter of a million dollars apiece is quite okay. I'll have the cash for us this afternoon.'

The nine of his warriors who had been at the chateau breathed a sigh of relief. Four of them had pledged this sum to the Prophets for the privilege of entering the internal group. The Prophets themselves had described it as a goodwill gesture. In fact the scene had been somewhat tense. *If you entrust us with the welfare of your souls, you must also entrust us with the welfare of everything else – everything.* Miraculously, legal papers had then appeared signing over to the Prophets of the Prophet movement the control of vast sums of oil investment capital. The Pashmanis had no such capital to transfer, but their offer of a 'little present' of a million dollars had been sufficient. *But only for four of you.*

Two thirds of the people there had not given anything – not because they did not want to, but because they could not. Their only feeling had been one of the most profound guilt, and a few had gone down on their knees to beg entrance. They had been dealt with coldly and cynically. Their own 'little presents' of only tens of thousands of dollars had been grudgingly accepted.

'I, of course,' Qhe continued, 'will be going with you. And I shall take the place of . . .'

He looked carefully at the nine men to see whom he most resembled.

'. . . take the place of Milarepa.'

The warrior's face dropped for a second, but soon smiled as Qhe went on; 'And looking like me, you can be me while I'm gone. You must be nothing but regal!' he ordered in a German accent. All nine of the warriors chuckled. 'Now, there are other things to be done. Firstly, I want four of you to stick with Willard. I know he can look after himself, perhaps better than any of us, but I want to be certain. You're also to inform Pashman to have the priests put him in a special bubble. Also, they're to direct all their energies here.'

He produced a large map of Africa and indicated the point in the Sahara where the cube stood. He then pointed to one of his men, in fact a young boy of seventeen, who stepped forward to stand in front of Qhe.

'Pick this up very clearly,' Qhe said gently, taking the boy's hands. 'First, breathing calmly. Everything gentle, everything smooth. Now let the energies rise gradually, gradually, gradually. Good. Open your mind's eye. Be passive, be soft, be receptive, be female, receive.'

In his own imagination, Qhe carefully recreated the image of the huge grey astral cube with the black cube in the ground at its centre. At the same time, he recreated its malevolent vibrations and texture. When it was perfectly fixed in his mind, he willed it to transfer into the boy's imagination and mind. They stood there quietly for two minutes as the transfer took place, the rest of the warriors helping by concentrating on soothing the atmosphere to facilitate the psychic exchange of information.

'I have it,' the boy said, now sweating slightly, and gulped theatrically. 'A bit heavy, isn't it?'

'A bit,' Qhe answered. 'I want our priests to work directly on the energy quality. I don't think they have a chance of dissipating it, but we need it just a bit more gentle, a bit more malleable. The last thing we need is a trace on the three Prophets.' He turned to the six men who had visited the chateau and were remaining in Europe. 'I want their backgrounds traced. I appreciate that their whole appearances may have changed, but I want them traced. Use clairvoyance and straightforward investigation. Get the two journalists to help, but remember that they're supposed to be dead. The photographer, Marie, incidentally is a sister – treat her as such. The man, Purot, may be a problem. If he is, put him to sleep until I get back. Okay? Are there any questions?'

'Why aren't we . . .' one of the warriors asked, 'just – er – destroying the movement?'

He asked the question with such gentleness and apparent sympathy that Qhe and his comrades roared with laughter. When the laughing had subsided, Qhe answered; 'They shall destroy it themselves – and we *shall* help. The energies they've created are such that if we shattered them, they would just disperse across the planet and still exist to work their evil. It has to be destroyed from within. It has to occultly cave in upon itself. It has to be sucked back up.'

'And how shall we do this?'

'I will tell you afterwards,' Qhe replied very slowly, '– when I know.'

The expressions on the faces of the group of thirty men and women were intense and excited. They stood nervously in the airport hall waiting for their private chartered flight to be called. They were all experienced travellers, but they had never been on a trip like this. Their destination remained a mystery, but they knew that there they would meet him, *him* – the man promised by the Prophets, the man promised by all the world scriptures, the man who would come again to judge, to avenge and to right the planet. The miracles that the three Prophets had performed were nothing compared to what this man would do. He was supreme. He was excellent. He was divine. And this group would do anything to serve him – anything.

Qhe and his three warriors also wore this expression of intense devotion. They looked as innocently demented as the rest of them. Qhe had not been recognized because of his close resemblance to the Pashmani whom he had replaced. Like his three compatriots, he wore a sober dark grey lounge suit, a white shirt and tie. Of everything the tie annoyed him beyond belief – it made him feel that he was about to become the victim of a lynch mob. It also annoyed him to have to wear the sickly intense look of expectant devotion. Yet there was a certain humour in it all that kept him inwardly gleeful.

Twitching nervously, he walked across to the bookstall

and bought a copy of the *International Herald Tribune*. Headline news was the frantic buying and selling that was suddenly taking place on the international money market. Both the Bank of England and the Central Bank of Italy had been forced to begin selling gold reserves to cover the drop in the value of sterling and the lira. Qhe winced slightly at the news and his previous feeling of inward glee was replaced by one of worried impatience. Oh Lord, he thought, this affair had to be played so carefully when every instinct in his body urged him just to rush in and destroy the evil. He inhaled deeply and sighed noisily.

'It's all right, brother,' one of the Arab travellers sympathized. 'We all feel the same way.'

Qhe looked up hesitantly and smiled. What a horrible joke, he thought, what a horrible bloody joke. A few seconds later the flight was called and the party walked solemnly across the tarmac to the small passenger jet. As the plane took off, half the passengers began reciting passages from the Koran and the rest closed their eyes in silent prayer. Qhe's three warriors also began to chant, but theirs was a hymn of joy that told of a battle between a devil and an angel – the devil lost the fight and became a milkmaiden. Qhe smiled wryly at their humour and glanced at his watch. He reckoned the flight would take about five hours and there was nothing better to do than sleep. All he asked was not to remember his dreams.

He pushed back his seat and closed his eyes. Almost immediately the flickering images of Pashman and his palace came into his imagination. The glittering white marble, the priests, his wives sitting crosslegged in the shape of the seven-pointed star, his son now six months old being cradled and suckled by his mother. This picture of his son melted his heart and soothed his stomach. He could spend a lifetime playing with and loving this boy, this tiny sun-god. To the sound of his three warriors still singing their song, he fell asleep.

He woke almost five hours later to the noise of completely different music. Strange organ music was being played over the aircraft's internal tannoy system. The tune was pleasant enough, the tempo was pleasant enough, but there was something macabre in the construction of the chords and harmonies. Just as some music elevates the spirit or makes one joyful or aggressive, so this music was composed and constructed to quiet the mind and yet to make the emotions tingle with a strange expectancy.

Even Qhe, as he woke, was caught by its vibrations and, for only a moment, thought how *pleasant* it was before realizing its sinister effect. He looked immediately to his three compatriots who nodded back that they understood what was happening. Then he looked around the cabin at the faces of the other men and women. Their eyes blazed back at him. They did not know what was happening, but they sensed what to them was an incredible glory.

As the plane began to bank and descend, the music became louder and stronger, and the passengers began to mindlessly nod their heads in time with it. Even before they had landed, they were caught in a web of magic that made everything seem mysterious and miraculous.

Then one of them gasped.

'Look, look!' he said anxiously, pointing out of his porthole.

Below them, in the middle of the burning yellow sand of the Sahara, they could see the hollow with the huge gleaming black cube at its centre. Their eyes rolled in wonderment at the bizarre sight. The volume and intensity of the music increased even more, and the plane was filled with the smell of a strange incense. It was a mixture of storax, musc and a third scent that was familiar, but which Qhe could not quite define. Then he almost smiled as he recognized it: tobacco. A blend of storax, musc and tobacco. It was lethal and he shook his head at the way in which everything was set up. How could the sanest man who knew nothing of magic be able to resist all this?

The plane landed smoothly and came to a halt. Immediately, the engines were cut and the music stopped, and there was an eery silence. For five minutes no one moved and nothing happened then, as if from nowhere, two men appeared on the runway pushing the steps for the aircraft's exit. They wore deep purple robes and gloves, and their heads were covered with purple gauze.

Once the steps had been fixed in position, one of the crew members appeared from the pilot's cockpit. He, too, was now dressed in purple and his face was covered. He swung open the doorway and silently indicated that the passengers should disembark. As they left the plane in total silence, they were struck by great blasts of heat frrom the burning desert. The sun and its reflection off the sands was dazzling and they blinked, temporarily blinded. When they had all descended there was the shrieking noise of the jet engines restarting and within two minutes the plane had taken off.

The small group of human beings stood pathetically alone. The steps and the two men who had pushed them had disappeared as mysteriously as they had appeared.

'Allah preserve us,' one of the men whispered.

'Preserve us, preserve us,' a woman echoed.

Slowly they became accustomed to the heat and glare of the sun. Able to focus and see clearly again, a sudden movement a quarter of a mile away attracted their attention. Another man dressed in purple had appeared, seemingly out of the sands, and stood waiting for them. The party began to move slowly across the desert towards him. Qhe and his men remained in the centre of the group, but he looked around searching for the whereabouts of the hollow and the cube now hidden by the undulating sand-dunes. He could not see it, but he could feel it and he knew that they were now within the vast astral cube which was invisible to his normal physical vision. He could find no words to describe the atmosphere of this place – it made his flesh and the flesh of his warriors creep.

The others, however, felt nothing but wonder. For them, it was all too magnificent. It was pure magic, pure sorcery, pure enchantment.

As they approached within a hundred yards of the man in purple, he disappeared, but when they reached where he had stood, they could see some steps carved from green marble descending into the ground. The group hesitated only for a second before beginning their descent.

Immediately beneath the earth's surface the temperature dropped and once again they could smell the incense of ambergris, musc and tobacco. The entire tunnel surrounding the steps was lined in green marble which possessed a strange luminous quality that lighted their way, but did not illuminate where the steps ended. They had descended almost seven hundred feet when the passageway began to widen and the incline of the steps lessened. Then they could hear running, rushing water and a little further on they came to a series of tiny waterfalls falling into two gutters that ran on either side of the tunnel. The water also had a green tint.

Further on the steps widened into a majestic one-hundred-foot-wide staircase now at least a thousand feet below the surface. Not one of the party stopped to hesitate or to turn around. They were held perfectly in the spell that enveloped them. Finally the steps ended and they were in a mammoth cavern, over two hundred yards long and with a ceiling a hundred yards high. Its walls were perfectly smooth and also lined in the phosphorescent green marble. The two streams that had rushed down either side of the steps now zig-zagged across the floor of the cavern forming an intricate pattern that could be crossed by small Japanese arched bridges.

There was still the smell of the incense and the air was cool, yet there was a strange texture to the atmosphere. Every moment and in every place that the eye turned it seemed as if lights and shapes were flickering in and out of sight, as though a hundred ghosts were dancing above their heads taunting the human visitors with only the slightest of glimpses.

Qhe could feel the mood of the party change from one of confident spiritual aspiration to one of primitive superstition. They walked more slowly now and they hardly dared to look around them. Their instincts, however, took them forward across the chamber, following a serpentine path that led across the arched bridges. Every step they took, the atmosphere seemed to become more weird and exciting. The shapes that were in the air became increasingly real and seemed to dance above their heads and in between them.

Suddenly the light tinkling noise of a silver bell could be heard ahead of them. Then it sounded behind them. A few seconds later it came from their right and then from their left, and then there was silence again. The phosphorescent glow from the ceiling and walls began to dim and soon they could hardly see their own hands. The bell began tinkling again and the air filled with hovering phantom forms of green, purple and scarlet. The temperature began to drop and the party shivered in the sudden cold.

The lighting returned to normal, the bells stopped and the phantoms disappeared, but only for a few seconds. As the party began to relax, it all began again, but infinitely more intensely.

The noise of bells was everywhere. The lighting went completely and everything was pitch-black broken only by the hovering luminous shapes that seemed to brush against the people's heads. Again, the lighting came on and the noise ended. A second later it was black once more. The innocent visitors were now terrified and held in a grasp of primeval superstitious fear. They could not move and stood rooted and trembling, not even daring to shout or even pray aloud.

The whole cavern rang with the noise of a thousand bells, shrilly pealing together so that finally they sounded like one single high-pitched note that pierced into the ears and minds of the party. The whispering shapes were actually touching their bodies, brushing against them like wisps of damp spiders' webs.

Their hair stood on end, their stomachs crept and they shook in the confusion, panic and horror of the moment. It lasted for five minutes as they were taken to the verge of their sanity.

'Stop! Stop! In the name of the Prophet, it ends!'

THIRTEEN

Within a split second the command had been obeyed. The darkness ended; the noise ended; the atmosphere ended. There was a sudden and overwhelming soothing tranquillity.

The party blinked and looked around for the person who had given the imperious order. The voice had been strangely shrill. They could see nothing until one of the men pointed to the far end of the cavern.

He stood there naked, not more than six years of age, a distant smile upon his face. His slim body was tanned and supple, and his face was that of a gilden cherub. His hair was long and dyed light violet. He looked confidently across the chamber.

'Everything,' he spoke, his voice echoing around the cavern, 'obeys the Prophet. Hither, come hither. All is well.'

In a state of semi-trance, the party moved towards him, the child who had saved them. Qhe and his warriors pretended to be similarly affected, but none of it had touched them. They had only been impressed by the carefully staged magical show. The child is a nice touch, Qhe thought to himself, showing real flair. The people around him would be ready to accept anything and to submit themselves to anything. The power of magic and suggestion was irresistible to those who were ignorant of its laws. In a situation like this the most intelligent and sophisticated of men were almost completely vulnerable if they were innocents to sorcery.

As they reached the end of the cavern, the child disappeared, but there was an archway through which they were obviously intended to pass. They went through it and then entered another tunnel that swung round to the left. In it were a dozen more naked young boys swinging incense burners.

'It is good to be cleansed for the Prophet,' one of them said gently.

'You must keep absolute silence,' said a second.

They walked through the row of violet-haired children and their bodies and clothes were soaked in the smoke of the perfume. They now entered a second cavern where a child indicated that they should remove their clothes and put on the purple robes that had been provided for them. On top of these they placed purple veils to cover their heads and faces. They then walked down yet another tunnel, this time lined with violet marble, where they were censed a second time. As they progressed down it, the temperature began to rise until they were sweating profusely beneath their robes.

Again the atmosphere changed and there was a new scent in the air. It stupefied and made them dizzy and they began to stumble. There was a drug permeating the air and its physical effect hit Qhe and his warriors as much as it touched the others. Qhe swore inwardly as he felt his body losing control and his head begin to spin from the effect of the opiated incense. He looked round to make certain that his warriors were all right, but could not find or recognize them because of the veils of purple gauze.

He stood still for a second, centering his mind above his body in order to send out a psychic call to his three men. Once centred, however, his attention was immediately focused on something else. He realized for the first time – and it was a realization that made him shudder at its implications – that they were all within some vast body of astral consciousness. He remembered the way in which the tentacle had come probing out from the astral cube to take him, attracted purely by his vibration that held too much light. Now he was inside it, in its very core, a single vibration of light from him would inevitably commence a process that could psychically squash him to instant death.

He remained silent, carefully and gently feeling his way around him. Who had created this? How had it been created? Was it a life all of its own or was it controlled? Was the informing energy human or from the other side?

His mind raced on these questions as he attempted to correctly orientate himself for action. But for what action?

The party stepped out of the tunnel and found themselves in burning sunlight and a few hundred feet away from the shining black cube that now towered above them. Two more naked boys appeared, dancing and tripping their way towards them. They grabbed the robes of one of the visitors and began to spin him around. Their faces smiled and seemed to giggle, but they emitted no noise of any kind. They moved on and began to spin a second visitor. Then some more boys appeared, dancing wildly in and out of the group, making the people spin and twist. Within a few minutes, fifty of these strange children had arrived and soon everyone was spinning and dancing with them.

The energies and movements intensified until they were all held and moving in wild frenzied action. The atmosphere was approaching that similar to the climax of an orgy, but there was no sex or violence. As it reached its psychic orgasm, the boys fell to the ground as one, clutching at the visitors' legs and knees, pulling them also to the earth. They fell easily, their opium-soaked brains willing to do and follow anything. There was silence and calm for a few minutes, and then the children buried their faces in the ground, indicating that the visitors should do likewise.

'Don't look up,' one of them whispered anxiously. 'Whatever you do, don't look up.'

They were filled with an incredible sense of anticipation and then they knew, they felt that someone was walking among them. His steps were careful and gentle, and they could hear his robe brushing against the ground and occasionally touching their bodies. There was a strange odour about him, something infinitely magical – and they did not dare to turn their eyes up from the ground.

'I bless you, little followers,' a deep resonant voice chanted at them.

One of the visitors, an Arab who helped control the oil money from Kuwait, could not stop himself. Twitching nervously in hysterical expectation, he looked up.

'You!' the great voice chanted and the Arab saw only a

hand pointing down at him.

It seemed as if a stream of energy were pouring from the hand and he crumpled back unconscious to the earth. Everyone could sense what had happened and they were filled with an even greater awe. Qhe desperately restrained his immediate instinct to hurl some energy back at this man, to look up and confront him, and trembled slightly in the moment.

'You are right to feel this awe,' the voice chanted at Qhe. 'Your trembling is a sign of adoration. You are chosen.'

A half-dozen of the boys immediately pounced on Qhe and lifted him from the ground to spin him around and around, and then to lead him off. With the opium, the spinning, the children like pestering wasps and the heat, Qhe was not able to focus on the owner of the voice. A few seconds later he found himself in the cool of another chamber.

'You have been chosen,' one of the children piped at him. 'Honour, honour, a great honour.'

Then he was left alone. He shook his head to clear his befuddled brain and sighed noisily. He began to reorientate himself when a second man from the party was led into the same chamber.

'You have been chosen,' the message was repeated. 'Honour, honour, a great honour.'

Qhe moved immediately to lift the man's purple veil and was greeted by a pair of eyes, blazing in the bliss and joy of the moment. It was not one of his warriors. Over the next few minutes, three more men and one woman were brought in, all in the same state. The one thing they had in common, Qhe knew, was that they were the most intense and devotional of the group – similar, Qhe suddenly thought, to the dying people whom Willard had seen in the clinic near Geneva. At least that's one mystery we'll soon solve, he thought cynically.

Meanwhile the rest of the party had been led away from the black cube and into a separate chamber. It was as vast as the very first cavern which they had entered, but the walls of this one were lined with luminous blue marble. At its end was a small lake at the centre of which was a platform with a white marble throne upon it. There was also a different incense being burned and there was the sound of distant gongs and chimes being rung. The group was instructed by a child to sit crosslegged by the lake and facing the throne. The tempo and volume of the gongs and chimes increased, creating a rhythm that made the party want to stand and dance, but they had been ordered to remain crosslegged and so they remained. They did not, however, have to sit there long for as the tension began mounting inside them two groups of boys appeared on either side of the lake.

They came forward dancing and throwing petals onto the water. There was an infectious gaiety about their movement and the group began to clap in time with their movement. And then, from the right, *he* appeared. There was no mistaking him. There could be no deception. He stood six feet six inches tall and was magnificently built with huge shoulders and rippling muscles. He was naked except for a purple kilt like a Roman gladiator's and a gold sash that crossed his chest. His hair and beard were of a deep golden colour, and hung in ringlets down his back and chest. The features of his face could have been chiselled from granite.

He strode across the cavern not looking once in the direction of the party and, without a moment's hesitation or care, continued striding across the water of the lake as if it was a material as the earth itself. He reached the massive white marble throne, stood by it for a second, then sat. He did not move for a full five minutes and looked intently over at the group. For them, he was the most beautiful and impressive man they had ever seen. No, he was more than a man. He was like unto a god. It seemed as if there were a shimmering silver halo all around him. Indeed he was perfection. He was what every man should strive to be. The group melted in his stare, all except the three Pashmanis who concentrated to hold a barrier of psychic electricity between themselves and this . . . they did not know what he was. A formidable sorcerer for certain, but more than that they could not tell. They trusted implicitly that their king,

Qhe, would be more than a match for him.

'Need I say anything?' his voice suddenly boomed across the water to them. 'Need I say a word? Do you need more than just to see the truth – the truth in me? I am the truth. Know it.'

His voice was so powerful and so powerfully vibrated that the listeners literally shuddered at his words. He then stood and gave them all the most beautiful smile of blessing. They were caught in the immediate radiance of his beam and felt themselves swallowed up by it. Instinctively they moved from their crosslegged position to kneel in his direction and to lift their veils. His smile deepened. It was so striking that they could hardly bare to look up at him and one by one their heads dropped.

It was at this precise moment that Qhe and the five others were led each one by a small boy into the cavern. The vibration of hysterical devotion in the five had increased as their emotions had played back on each other. As they entered the first thing they saw was all their comrades kneeling forward with expressions of total bliss. They then looked across the water to the throne and *him*. The woman and one of the men gasped and their footsteps began to fail, but they were still led carefully forward by the boys. Staggering like the others, Qhe looked coldly through his veil at the man. Mister Hercules, he thought sarcastically to himself, Mister Universe himself. So skirts were coming back into fashion eh?

He did not allow himself the pleasure of these real thoughts for longer than a second as he had to behave in perfect harmony with the other five. There was, however, the most bizarre atmosphere in the cavern. There was something there, something happening that could not be seen by the physical eye. It could, though, be sensed and it was something far more sinister than just the atmosphere or the intense devotion to the pyschic Tarzan on his throne.

It was familiar to Qhe and he knew that he had experienced it before, but where and when he could not remember. He let his body mechanically follow the other five as they moved to stand in front of their kneeling comrades right at the water's edge. Qhe looked down into the water without focusing and it was then that he recalled perfectly what there was about the atmosphere. It stank of the aura of a ceremonial black magician. The air was filled with invisible malicious denizens of the spirit worlds. Now that he remembered, he could feel their evil, cunning power. Astral creatures, astral blobs of malevolent energy, devils and demons.

This whole place was a playground and shrine of evil spirits. Qhe knew that if he were out of his body and fully clairvoyant, he would be able to see a vast throng of these involutionary entities watching and aiding the affair, giving the man on the throne their power and energy.

Now the man who was the Prophet stood and opened wide his arms in blessing. A flash of energy shot forth from his to surround Qhe and the five others. He closed his arms and then opened them again, repeating the movement eight times in all, building up the wave of energy to the six people before him. Then his hand traced a sign in the air before him, the signature of a demon, and then he traced seven more. All the time, however, his face continued radiating this magnificent beaming smile into the eyes of his devotees. To them it seemed only that he was giving them all the most marvellous, divine blessing. Except for the four Pashmanis, they had no idea at all of what was truly taking place.

With his arms outstretched, the Prophet now took a step forward. The devotees trembled – *he* was approaching them. His eyes looked piercingly into each of the six who stood closest to the water and Qhe immediately felt the energy round his own stomach being drawn to the man. At the same time, telepathically, Qhe heard the man saying: *come to me, come to me, give me your energy*. He took another step towards them and his radiant smile broadened. Now even to the ordinary physical eye the shimmering energy could be seen coming from his hands, shooting out to and around them.

Yet another step forward and the Prophet was standing on the water.

'Love me,' his terrific voice resounded across the water and around the cavern. 'Love me.'

Give me your force, however, was the message that Qhe felt as he sensed the very electric fibre of his own body being drawn away from him and to the prophet. The five others at Qhe's side were in a state of total bliss and had completely surrendered themselves to the Prophet. They let all their emotions, all their energy, all their psychic power flow out to the man. Qhe, too, felt everything being sucked from him and now commenced a desperate battle to stop the process from emptying him. If he moved or shouted or did anything, he would break the spell of the Prophet and be safe, but he had to remain as mindless and as apparently blissed out as the five others in order not to be discovered.

As he breathed in, he imagined himself holding in all the energy around him. As he exhaled, he willed a solid curtain of electricity into existence to protect himself. It was as if he were in the very centre of the vortex of a gigantic psychic vacuum cleaner, a huge invisible vampire that was menacingly attempting to suck away his very soul. He felt himself totally alone within a cosmos whose sole object was to drain him of his self. The base of his spine began to quiver uncontrollably and he now fully understood what was happening. The Prophet was trying to steal away from him that dynamic charge of biological electricity that is the very core of the human body. Without that charge, the physical body just wastes away.

Nothing will be taken from me, Qhe said quietly to himself, and concentrated waves of calming energy down his body to the base of his spine. *Nothing, nothing, nothing.* Suddenly in his mind, he could hear a hundred taunting voices, telling him to *give, worship, submit, surrender*! He felt stabbing pinpricks of pain in his skull and down his body, all of which were trying to distract his attention. *It is God's will that you give in, give away, submit, surrender!* Qhe's power of concentration ignored these provoking words and physical jibes from the vicious spirits, and looked to the Prophet to see if he realized that Qhe was resisting.

Totally confident of his supreme power, the Prophet could not even conceive that he might fail and was blind to Qhe. He had worked this spell with hundreds of people and, with the aid of his spirits, had never failed.

The Prophet's smile now became ecstatic as he felt the dynamic living energy of the five devotees being drawn into him. He raised his hands to the sky and dropped them. He then took another step forward on the water.

'I,' he boomed, 'am well pleased with you. You serve me and will continue to serve me. You are my chosen children. I, the Prophet of all ages, He who is the chosen one of the Lord, of God, of Allah, of the Infinite, I have come again. Soon you will behold me walk openly upon the face of the planet again and you will be my chosen disciples. The new order will come and his divine will once more imprinted upon humanity. You serve me. And I serve the infinite divine. Go in peace. Guard your silence. Await the signs. Give of everything you have to fulfil the divine will. Bless you, my children. Bless you.'

The radiant smile on his face disappeared, he turned his back on them and strolled casually across the water to disappear through a tunnel at the far end of the cavern.

The devotees were given no time to absorb what had happened for immediately fifty dancing children appeared to lead them away. They were taken back through the tunnels and other chambers, but now there was no music or incense. Ten minutes later, they were changing back into their ordinary clothes and, twenty minutes later, they were walking back up the steps of the runway. They had not been there for longer than three hours. The speed and intensity of the experience affected them like a psychic nuclear explosion. For a while even Qhe was stunned by the speed with which the whole scene had taken place and how they were now being rushed away.

His three warriors walked beside him, waiting still for their king to order them into action. He looked at them and smiled calmly to reassure them all was well, but his mind was racing to decide on what he had to do. Whichever way he faced the situation there seemed to be only one solution

– and it was an answer that made his stomach turn to even think of it. There was no choice for him, no choice at all.

'Go back with them,' he whispered to his warriors. 'What I must do, I can only do alone. All will be well, believe me. Only tell Willard that the three Prophets of the Prophet must be exposed – exposed as soon as possible. Tell him that it does not matter how, but that it must be done.'

He quickly took each one of his three men's hands and brushed his lips across them.

'Pray for me,' he whispered.

Then screaming wildly and with the fury of total mania, he began to run back down the steps to the cavern.

FOURTEEN

Knocking aside the children as if they were flies, Qhe sprinted six steps at a time back down into the ground. The children screamed at him to stop and the rest of the party watched him non-comprehending. For a second, a few of them instinctively tried to follow, but their way was blocked by the three warriors who shepherded them back up the steps and over the desert to the waiting aircraft.

Qhe reached the cavern with the zig-zag pattern of streams and hurdled across the waters to the far side. As he entered the tunnel to take him into the next cavern, he was confronted by three human beings who were not small children. They stood tall and menacing in their purple robes. Screaming again, Qhe hurtled towards them at the last moment throwing himself in the air and over their heads. He landed in a rolling somersault and continued running.

He entered a small cavern which he had not previously seen and knew that he was lost, but he kept running letting his instinct guide him. He was confronted by a second group of men, but again he threw himself over their heads. He sprinted like this for over twenty minutes until finally he found himself once again in the cavern with the lake and throne. He rushed to the exit where the Prophet had disappeared, but found his way blocked by thirty small boys and a dozen adults.

He stopped dead and instantly calmed his breathing. All the energy that had been pulsing and speeding while he ran was still rushing through his body. In a moment of supreme willed concentration, he forced the energy up through his body and into his hands and eyes. He then hurled the energy like bullets at the skulls of the men and boys who barred his passage. They immediately grasped their heads, overcome by intense pain like a migraine, and Qhe walked calmly past them.

The tunnel down which he passed wove like a serpent through the rock and its walls were grey and dimly lit. Qhe shuddered at the sight that greeted him in the next chamber. It was filled with the macabre accessories of a medieval sorcerer: huge cages containing savage wild rats, toads and vampire-bats; bottles containing leeches, eagles' feathers, slugs, dried snakes and lizards; row upon row of different kinds of incense and perfume. The next chamber was filled with astrological equipment, the walls covered with charts. Qhe examined one closely and his nose twitched at the horrible odour of the parchment made of stretched human skin. All the astrological calculations followed the dark courses of the moon and stars, and also in this room were dried and sickly herbs.

Qhe walked through into the next chamber where were robes of every conceivable colour and design, all of them, however, heavy with the aura of darkness. He started as a rat darted across the floor and touched his feet. Past this chamber, he entered yet another tunnel which was narrower than any of the others. Here hovered the acrid smell of burning sulphur and animal blood, and Qhe knew that he was coming closer to the Prophet. Inwardly, he steeled himself for anything. He could not afford to surround himself in a bubble of light and instead created a series of tiny crosses and pentacles in each of the seven electric centres of his body – the seven chakras from the base of his spine through the generative centre, the solar plexus, the heart, the throat and the centre of the forehead, to the top of his skull. This would at least afford him some invisible protection.

The tunnel twisted and turned for several hundred feet until finally it reached its opening. Qhe carefully stepped through it and could scarcely believe his eyes. In that one day he had seen enough strange things but nothing as weird as what lay before him now.

There was yet another cavern, far larger than any of the others, a quarter of a mile in width and length. From its roof hung a vast army of gleaming silver-grey stalactites.

Qhe had come out at an entrance that almost touched this roof and he could have reached out to hold one of these mineral icicles. Below him, carved steps wove their tortuous way down to the base of the cavern which was covered by thousands of stalagmites reaching up, some of them forty feet into the air.

Fifty or so small fires were burning, lighting the cavern with their macabre glow and casting eery flickering shadows. A clearly discernable path led through the stalagmites to the opposite side where the Prophet, now wearing only a tattered grey cloak over his magnificent body, sat huddled against the wall. He looked up at Qhe with the cunning of a vulture and, though four hundred yards away, Qhe could see his eyes glinting red in the firelight.

Qhe slowly descended the steps into this hell on earth. The drop to the floor below was over three hundred feet and he held himself close to the rock face; a fall would mean instant death impaled on the sharp point of a stalagmite. After only a few steps, he realized that there was a thought in his mind which was urging him to jump. He smiled and hurled the thought back at the prophet. A few seconds later his mind echoed with the idea that he was afraid of heights, that he was becoming dizzy, that he was swaying, that he was falling. *Jump!* he was told. Qhe smiled again. Even at the age of five, he had been too strong for suggestions such as those.

Throwing off the thoughts like a dog shaking off water, he continued down the steps. Suddenly as if from nowhere a dozen men appeared fifty feet ahead of him. They stood casually upon the steps at five-yard intervals, looking calmly but intensely at him. He looked at them for a few seconds and then pretended to back away. As he did so, he appeared to sway and immediately received what he wanted. Once more the thought that he was afraid of heights and that he should jump rang through his mind as the Prophet willed the energy at him.

Now, instead of instantly throwing these thoughts back at the Prophet, Qhe began to absorb them. For fifteen seconds, he pretended to sway and let them accumulate in and around him. Then, with the same ease that a tennis player can deflect a ball, Qhe made the thoughts ricochet off him and down to the first man who barred his way. The man looked as if an enormous hand had suddenly grabbed him and hurled him into the air, and he dropped like a stone to the floor. Qhe did not stop to see how he had landed, but deflected the energy again at the second man who barred his way. He, too, threw himself instantly into the air. A third and a fourth man fell similarly. A look of total confusion on his face, the fifth man clung frantically to the rockface and Qhe danced past him.

A surge of victorious energy running through him, Qhe actually pirouetted and spun in the air, emitting a blood-curdling Pashmani warrior's cry. The sixth man grasped and missed. The seventh received a vicious kick in the knees and found himself hanging from the steps. The eighth stepped meekly back. The ninth and the tenth prepared themselves to attack, but once again Qhe threw the Prophet's own energy at them. They shuddered and twitched as an irresistible urge to jump passed through them. One of them hovered on the edge, swaying backwards and forwards, and Qhe slipped neatly between him and the rock-face. The other hurled himself face down on the steps and Qhe stepped gingerly over his body.

Now there remained only the eleventh and twelfth, but these two had been instructed in sorcery and knew what was happening. They linked hands and their eyes blazed at Qhe. Immediately Qhe lifted his own hands, blocking their eyes from view and turning their energy back on them. They willed their force through the intruder's hands and into his body, but they had no chance. His hands created a mirror-like shield and the total venom of their destructive energy was being thrown back at them.

Qhe waited a few seconds and then, just for an instant, spat some of his own force at them through his hands. They recoiled back as if a steamroller had hit them and in the next second, Qhe was past them.

He ran down the rest of the steps and along the path that led through the stalagmites to the Prophet. A thousand different images were thrown up to enter his mind, to distract and stop him. Monsters of the most hideous kind flashed before his eyes. Divinely beautiful naked women voluptuously invited him to join an orgy with them. He saw pictures of his own mutilated dead body moulding among swarming flies and ants. The stalagmites turned into huge menacing trees that threatened to suck him from the ground. The ceiling seemed to lower itself and the walls begin to cave in on him. An actual stalactite fell from the air burying itself deep in the ground in front of him. Yet still he kept running along the path. Nothing – no nightmare real or imagined – could prevent him from moving forward.

At last he was within two hundred feet of the Prophet who now stood and threw off his cloak. He was strangely impressed by the way this pathetic human creature had managed to reach him and he raised his hand to prevent the sixty more men who lay hidden around him from attacking and destroying the man.

Qhe stopped running and began to walk slowly. He could sense the hidden men, but he kept his eyes fixed rigidly on the face of the Prophet. Fifty feet away, he stopped and fell to his knees.

'Master, master,' Qhe cried, 'I mean no harm. I want only to serve, to serve you, to serve.'

In a position of abject and humble worship,

FIFTEEN

'Kiss them again!' the Prophet intoned.

Once more Qhe humbly lowered his head and brushed his lips across the man's feet.

'And again. And again. And again.'

Qhe continued his servile embraces, but when the fourth order came, he suddenly withdrew.

'No!' Qhe shouted. 'I am not come to be your slave, but your servant. Truly, I can serve you well.'

The Prophet stroked the curls of his beard and smiled.

'You? You think you dare to know that you can serve me? Have you not seen my power? Do you not know that I have taken your life force and that you are bound to die, to waste away.'

'Oh master,' Qhe answered with feeling, 'I have seen your power, but I held back my life force from you. You plucked the five others, but I protected myself. How could a dying man serve you?'

The Prophet's eyes narrowed and he looked piercingly down at Qhe. Qhe looked back and held the man's stare. He did not fight the man's intense glare, but absorbed it gently focusing his attention on the Prophet's forehead. The Prophet himself now willed all his power through his eyes, but still Qhe did not flinch or blink or look away. The Prophet's expression changed for he had never met a being who could calmly look him back. It impressed him – and it worried him. He still, however, continued to look piercingly at Qhe. After three minutes of fraught silence, Qhe finally did blink and lowered his eyes.

'You are,' he said diplomatically, 'too powerful for me, oh Master.'

The Prophet smiled again and nodded sagely. This intruder was indeed strong – but no threat.

'Kiss my feet again,' he ordered.

Qhe looked up and sadly shook his head.

'If you have no other use for me then kill me now. Put me out of my misery. My whole life has been a journey to find you. Reject me and I shall gladly embrace death. Master,' he said plaintively, 'let me serve.'

'Why?' asked the Prophet coldly.

'So that I may learn and that I may share your future glory.'

'You want a lot,' the Prophet roared. 'Will you not kiss my feet again?'

Again sadly, Qhe shook his head.

'In God's name, I should destroy you,' the Prophet threatened.

'Your power,' Qhe answered with a look of clever and obvious cunning, 'comes not from God, but from Spirits. There is no God! Master, I am a worthy servant. Nowhere, nowhere will you find a man like me to serve you. Let me be your left hand and your left eye. Let me be your shadow and your human phantom. You *see* me. I know that your power *sees* me.'

The Prophet's look became gentler and Qhe knew that his psychic game of chess was beginning to work. Every atom in his self made him want to leap forward and throttle the huge carcass of evil, but he held his stance of servile arrogance.

'From childhood,' Qhe continued, 'I have been instructed in the arts of sorcery. In the East, there is no man who is my equal. I am the king of a nation. I move across the globe, playing my games, warping and changing the energies. I have acted alone and supreme in the knowledge that I am one of the monarch sorcerers. But you, oh master, oh lord, you make my actions look like those of a child. Beside you I am impotent and worthless. Beside you I am –'

'– you are Qhe?' the Prophet interrupted.

'I am.'

The Prophet's smile broadened into a grin, then a chuckle and then a volcano of laughter.

'And I had thought to be careful of you!' the Prophet exclaimed. 'Of you! I knew that what I heard was too good to be true. Obstruct me, I thought. You and all your praying priests.'

He roared with laughter again and Qhe watched him closely. He was beginning to see something and to hear something that he had not known before. As he looked at the figure and face of this herculean man, it seemed as if his flesh began to melt away and distort and mould into a different shape. The skin grew long and haggard and fell in aged folds from a thin and wizened face. The muscles of his body drooped and sagged and wilted into the pathetic frame of a tiny shrivelled old man.

The Prophet stopped laughing, knowing that Qhe was now seeing *him*. He breathed in deeply and Qhe's image of the shrivelled old man disappeared to once again be replaced by the beautiful torso and gleaming bronzed skin. Yet Qhe looked around at the murky grey atmosphere broken by the flickering flames of the fires. He smelled the scent of the sulphur and burning blood. He saw the tattered grey cloak and remembered the way in which this Goliath had sat huddled against the rockface when first he had entered this cavern.

'Do you think you can see me?' the Prophet asked, again laughing. 'You see only a tenth of the truth. And I wonder if I should trust you.'

In answer Qhe outstretched his arms and lay spread-eagled on the ground in front of the Prophet. He felt the Prophet move to stand directly over him, but did not flinch. He calmed his body totally so that not a single vibration came from it and made himself completely receptive and submissive. He felt the man probing him psychically and allowed the malevolent tentacles of perception to reach deep within him. Qhe swallowed to prevent himself vomiting at the horrible sensation of giving over his body for this disgusting examination. With his mind, he evoked a sensation of adulation and adoration which he coldly transferred to the man of evil.

The Prophet looked down and frowned. He felt a sense of doubt, yet overwhelming this was a feeling of supreme conceit. Here indeed was a man worthy to be his servant. A renowned white magician in complete submission to him. Here indeed was someone who could fully appreciate and applaud his manic scheme. Here indeed was a shadow who would lend added magnificence. But, still there was that doubt, that lingering doubt.

Qhe was supremely aware of the Prophet's hesitation.

'Wondrous Master, magnificent Master,' Qhe began to chant. 'You for whom my whole life has searched. You are the planet and the cosmos. You are all knowledge, all wisdom, all power. Before you everything gives way. Before you everything adores, everything worships, everything obeys. The world is a pawn in your hands. Men are ants beneath your feet. Spirits speed to fulfil your commands. Master of all. Lord of all...'

Qhe continued this chant of absolute adoration, playing on the man's monumental ego like a master musician. He was subservient and slavish, boot-licking and ingratiating, then courting and caressing, cajoling and adulating. For the Prophet this was the sweetest music in the world. He could not resist. Never had any man seen him so clearly, adored him so perfectly, served him so beautifully. Not for one second could he think that the adoring man at his feet was either acting or lying, because every word that Qhe said was the truth. Men were ants beneath his feet! The world was a pawn in his hands! He was the master of the planet and cosmos! Soon every man on earth would know this for the truth!

'... accept me, accept me,' Qhe finally ended his song of praise.

The Prophet was glowing once again and beaming his radiant smile down at Qhe. And Qhe knew that he had him like a butterfly in a net. Not for one second now would he relax the energy and hour by hour he would become ever more indispensable to the Prophet's evil egomaniacal vision of himself.

'And how, my little child,' the Prophet asked soothingly, 'would you serve me?'

'Master, I have already begun,' he answered still on his knees. 'Those puppets who are your three Prophets to the world – I have already destroyed two journalists who would have tried to warp their work and your plan. That group of hyenas, whom you allow to control your wealth – their greed is such that they might think to try and deceive you. Already, my most trusted servant has joined their group to guard over it for you. His adoration for you is as mine. I have warriors and my own knowledge of the workings of men's minds and the ways of their power. All this is yours. Only let me serve.'

'And in return?'

'Just to be with you. Just to bask in the rays of your wisdom and power, and learn.'

The Prophet's radiant smile became even more glorious, but Qhe, watching, saw once again the vision of a withered old man – a withered old man enveloped in demonry and witchcraft, surrounded by spirits and possessed children, bidding to fulfil a nightmare of sickening power.

SIXTEEN

The French police and the international agents for Interpol could do nothing. There were no warrants out for the men involved nor did they appear to be actually doing anything illegal. The conference of international Mafia chiefs was, however, making them shudder.

Two floors of the Georges V Hotel in Paris had been booked and the area was filled with men who wore silk suits and belonged to shooting and pistol clubs, and were therefore legally carrying firearms. There was also the added peculiarity of Monsieur Willard attending this meeting. The Family on its own was one thing. Qhe on his own was one thing. But put the two together and it was a thought to make every security man on the planet hang up his holster and retire to a monastery.

Added to that was the extra complication of the Prophets of the Prophet Movement. Place all this together and you had religion, money, crime ... It did not bear thinking about. All that the police could do was to pray that the conference would go smoothly and then pretend that it had never taken place. The only people with the slightest idea of what was taking place were the few attached to the central banks and high government officials who knew that international currency dealing was also involved – dealing that was about to fatally attack sterling unless that investigation into Trusts International Incorporated was called off.

But no one could make any sense of it all.

Willard carefully timed his entrance to take place after all the Dons were already in the executive suite that was being used for the conference. As always, he was his immaculately cool self. Although it was mid-summer and Paris was sweltering, he was still an unmistakable Englishman in his three-piece pinstripe suit and his umbrella in hand. He had made a point of coming to the city alone and having no bodyguards with him in the hotel; it added that final touch to his image. The Pashmani warriors were anyway deeply involved in trying to dig up the roots of the three Prophets.

As Willard strolled casually down the corridor to the executive suite, he thought for a second of the description the three warriors had given him of that place in the Sahara and the man who was the Prophet of the three Prophets. The image of Qhe running screaming back down the steps had stuck in his mind and he wished his dear brother the greatest safety in the world.

He nodded nonchalantly to the hoods who guarded the door and they grunted before opening it for him. He entered the room and looked slowly around, God, he thought to himself, what a cesspool of bloody sharks. Seated around the long oval table, already in a fog of cigar smoke, were the twelve Dons, their thousand-dollar watches, cufflinks and tie-clips sparkling in the sunlight that came through the window.

Don Gillamo, who sat at the end of the table, was the first to stand. Reluctantly and slowly, the others stood as well – a display of courtesy and respect for their new business partner. How long he would remain their associate, however, was something on which they had not yet decided.

'Good afternoon, gentlemen,' Willard said politely. 'I'm extremely pleased to meet you all. It's a pleasure, a great pleasure.'

'Jeesusss,' one of the Dons sighed, 'a limey! We've got to do business with a limey.'

'Business is business,' another whispered, 'so just shuddup, huh.'

Willard smiled as if he had not heard a word and took his seat at the end of the table opposite Gillamo. For just a moment he felt like Alice visiting the Mad Hatter's tea party in Wonderland.

'If I might begin?' Gillamo asked.

'Sure.'

'Start.'

'Shoot.'

'This meeting,' he started, 'is called under unusual circumstances and is for two purposes. First of all, gentlemen, it's to introduce you to our new business associate –'

'I thought,' a Don with a heavy New York accent interrupted, 'that our new associate was – er – an oriental gentleman of – er – how shall I put it? – a different skin colouring to our own. Like, where the hell is he?'

'I represent him every way, gentlemen,' Willard answered immediately. 'I reflect his opinions and decisions in all matters. As for his whereabouts, I shall come to that later. Shouldn't we for the moment, however, keep to our agenda?'

'Agenda!' the man from New York snorted. 'Since when . . .'

'Mister Willard is correct. This *is* a business meeting and I'm sure that his word is good enough for me.' The speaker was a small man who squinted and wore extremely thick-lensed spectacles. In his left hand was an electronic pocket calculator, in his right, a bottle of pills, tranquillizers. 'My name is Goldino, Mr Willard. I represent the family's interests on Wall Street and in Tokyo. I am certain that we shall understand each other very well.'

Willard bowed graciously to Goldino and smiled at the snake-like creature.

'I'm certain we shall,' Willard agreed.

'As I was saying,' Gillamo continued, 'our first purpose is to meet our new associate. Our second is to survey the situation in the light of this new circumstance and look to the future.'

'I'd like to say a few words first, Mister Chairman, just to ease our new associate into the picture. Is that all right, please?' The question was asked with laboured sarcasm by a huge man with a bullneck and huge shoulders. His hands were covered with dark hair and played incessantly with a rosary.

Gillamo nodded his approval and Willard turned his attention to this huge thug.

'My name,' the man continued, still in a threatening sarcastic tone, 'is Gordallini. And I represent the family for

Nevada and the West Coast of the United States, and specialize in our international leisure activities. And I would like Mister Willard to understand this: never in the history of the family has someone who is not a close relative become an associate. Of course, we make deals outside the family, but not in a hundred years has someone from outside come inside. Now, Don Gillamo was given full authority to run this operation, to make decisions, to do what's necessary. He is a Don like the rest of us, but just at the moment . . .' he smiled calmly at Willard, '. . . just at the moment, you understand, I don't think he could run a rest-home for corpses.'

There was silence for a few seconds as he let the words and their implication sink in. Willard nodded understandingly.

'Mr Willard,' Gordallini continued, 'if I had been running this razamataz . . . things would have been different, very different. You dig? But this is a family and we stick by the family. Yes? I'm sure you understand.'

The Dons looked to Willard for a reaction but he stared impassively back at them. After twenty seconds silence he shrugged and turned to Gordallini.

'You should know that your close relative, Gillamo, has already attempted to assassinate us twice – unsuccessfully as you can see. More than that, to perfectly illustrate his point His Majesty, Qhe, smoothly took over your villa fortress on the Riviera for a while. I can assure all you gentlemen that Don Gillamo's decision was one that any of you would have also taken. You should remember that it is purely politeness and a certain love for orderliness on our side that has prevented us . . . prevented us just pushing you aside. You may, for instance, own this hotel, gentlemen – but, if we wanted, we could own the city.'

He smiled and slowly looked at the men one by one. He had said everything with such perfect tranquillity that not one of them found it within himself to shout an objection.

'I'll grant you, however, gentlemen,' Willard continued, 'that you may consider all this a matter of opinion. I would only advise you *not* to put it to the test.'

The Dons were now seething with suppressed anger. Not even the Vice President of the United States had dared to talk to them like that. No one could get away with this.

'I think you've made your point,' Goldino, who ran Wall Street and Tokyo, finally said very quietly. His voice hissed a subdued venom. 'Can we get down to business?'

'Of course,' Willard answered. He, like Qhe in the Sahara, was playing all this by ear. He was an actor who had walked onto a stage not yet knowing his lines. One thing was obvious to him and that was that there was no way to seduce these men into willing co-operation. He was really going to have to make it worth their while – but how? He had at least one trump card up his sleeve.

'Firstly,' he began, 'we have already remedied a glaring loophole in your – I mean *our* – relations with the Prophets of the Prophet Movement. Your pride and business efficiency, gentlemen, did not seem to run to establishing relations with the man who actually runs the Movement. You seemed content to merely deal with his three lackeys in Europe. You will appreciate that that is no way to ensure a successful financial venture. Qhe is currently with *the* man who is behind the whole show.'

The Dons now looked furiously at Gillamo who shrugged and looked away embarrassed.

'There was no way,' Gillamo stuttered. 'I couldn't get a single lead on the cat.'

'That perfectly illustrates that you *do* need us, does it not?' Willard asked.

The snake, Goldino, was the first to nod his approval.

'Very shrewd,' he said.

'A double-cross,' another muttered.

'You had just better stick with us then,' Willard smiled.

'What else you got?' the man from New York asked. 'Is that the lot?'

Willard continued smiling impassively, but his mind was a blank a total blank. He did not panic, but continued sitting there as if he had every answer in the world. For almost a minute, there was silence.

'Give! Give!'

'If you're an associate, associate, goddammit!'

Willard's serene expression made every one of them certain that he was holding out on something. Only Willard knew that he was holding out on nothing. Then for some strange and irresistible reason, his mind was drawn back to their office in Marseilles, to the girl Marie, and to the sudden appearance of their visitor – that strange, enigmatic and beautiful visitor. That holy visitor had told them about the Plan for world economy and the threat posed to the International Monetary Fund conference, due now in only two weeks. At the same time, Willard also put into the picture the plan the Mafia had for destroying the pound sterling if they weren't allowed to keep their toe-hold in the United Kingdom.

His smile broadened.

'Goddammit, give!' he was told again.

'Certainly, gentlemen, certainly. It is only fair. Of everyone here you, Don Goldino, will appreciate its subtleties – and any others of you who understand world finance. Let us talk for a second about your threat to the Bank of England and other central banks. If they don't co-operate, you say, you will set their currencies spiralling down until they *do* co-operate, until they leave you alone to run your shady little businesses. You have missed the trees for the wood. You are in a position that every world financier would give his back teeth for. You have control, on behalf of the Prophets of the Prophet Movement, over vast blocks of capital, on which you can make vast profits by transferring it from currency to currency. What, however, you have forgotten is the International Monetary Fund Conference in Nairobi in two weeks. If this conference is successful, the sort of currency dealing about which I'm talking will become impossible. If, on the other hand, the conference fails – which it will if you carry out your threat – and if you make it fail because of an uncontrollable crisis, there will be absolute pandemonium on the finance market. You could clean up. You could triple what the Movement has already given you. It will have to be a carefully played game of snakes and ladders, but it would make all your other affairs look like child's play. When Qhe enters something like this, he enters to score – to score heavily.'

Willard looked meaningfully around at the Dons.

'You mean,' Goldini said, 'that you're going to ride your own money along with this?'

'All of it,' Willard answered simply. 'You understand that we could tie up everything – everything!'

Not saying another word, he stood and walked slowly from the room. The Dons looked around at each other, two trains of thought speeding through their minds.

'Can we handle this alone?' Gillamo asked.

'Those men have vision,' Goldino said with approval. 'It was kind of them to tell us.'

'Can we really score like that?'

'We can.'

'It's big.'

'The biggest.'

'Do we need them?'

'No.'

'And Qhe?'

'Who knows? We can sort him out later. This is one pie that we don't share.'

'Then we're agreed?' Gillamo looked carefully at each of his colleagues. They all nodded.

Gillamo now pressed a button and one of the bodyguards put his head around the door.

'Rub him out,' Gillamo ordered.

The man did not blink, but quietly closed the door behind him.

'Shall we get back to business,' Gillamo suggested, 'and work this all out?'

SEVENTEEN

Slightly bewildered by what he had said, Willard walked up the steps to the next floor in the hotel and along the corridor to his suite. Why, he asked himself, had he said all that? He was helping them to destroy the conference, helping them to make themselves and the movement infinitely richer and more powerful – *helping* them. And yet instinctively, he knew that somehow he had said the right thing, that somehow he was helping to weave a web that would entangle them until they were destroyed. But how?

He could only wait and see – and pray God that he was correct.

His stomach was tense and for the first time in twenty years he felt the beginnings of a headache. He would have a shower to clean off the vibrations of those men and then do an intense stint of yoga and meditation to put himself back together.

Still thinking about all this, he entered his suite and walked over to the window to draw the blinds. He then turned and found himself facing four men, each with a silenced revolver. Their faces were blank and their eyes icy cold. They stood at four-yard intervals and Willard's mind accelerated frenetically into full speed to take them on. No way, the voice in the back of his head told him. He could take on one and be hit by the other three. He had to use magic. He had to use sorcery. He had to get his energies rising and moving to stop these men.

But his stomach was tight and he had that infernal headache. His body, which was his only weapon, was not in working order. His mind sprang again to find a way of stalling them just to give him enough time to pull his forces together.

'This is the end of your line, buddy.'

Willard could do nothing but smile. Death did not for

one moment bother him. He knew too well that it was just a transfer from one state of being to another. All he would lose would be his physical body and, yes, he had a certain affection for it – but then again he might be more use without it. At least he would have no more stomach or headaches.

'Jolly good,' he said happily and closed his eyes to embrace death.

In that moment, he remembered how Qhe's mother had died. At the age of eighty, she had decided that she had had enough, that she had served her purpose and that her body was now just slowly wasting away. She asked her husband's approval, then Qhe's and then the priests'. They had all given her their blessing and she had commenced her fast. Seventeen days later, a blissful look on her face, she had left her body. That thought made Willard smile too as he waited for the thud of the silenced revolvers and the temporary pain.

He heard a thud, then a second and a third and a fourth, but he felt no pain, no wound in his body. Am I dead already? he asked himself. No, he answered himself, I appear to be still in my body. Do I not feel pain then? That's doubtful.

'Brother Willard,' he heard a voice whispering.

It was a familiar voice, a voice with a slight sing-song Pashmani accent.

'Brother Willard?' it came again.

Willard opened one eye a fraction and cautiously looked. A smiling Pashmani face greeted him. He opened the other eye and looked around the room. Four warriors dressed in the uniforms of hotel waiters stood over the dead bodies of the gangsters.

'Truly,' he said, 'I'm really most grateful.'

'You do not object to our interference?' came the polite reply.

'I'll just have to grin and bear it,' Willard answered and he and the four men laughed. 'Can you remove their bodies quietly?' he asked.

The men nodded.

'Let me have their guns first. I know what I want to do with them. Is there any news from Marseilles?'

'Yes, the research is almost complete, but I don't know what they've found.'

'Good. We'll go back immediately, but only after I've seen my new associates again.'

He picked up the four guns and placed them in a brown shopping bag. Then he left the suite and began to stroll back down to the conference room. He whistled and felt good. His stomach was calm again and his headache had gone. He was fond of miracles.

The guards on the door were well-trained professionals and did not betray any surprise at seeing the man who was supposed to have just been rubbed out. Willard gave them a wink before entering the room without knocking.

The Dons were still discussing the intricacies of the currency movements and had just decided to transfer the bulk of their own funds to the Prophets of the Prophet Movement accounts and investments. They were high on the enthusiasm created by the thought of such huge wealth. Their basic instincts of greed and power were being roused as never before. It was the heavy from New York who first noticed Willard standing in the doorway. His sudden silence and sour expression moved magnetically across the other Dons.

Willard looked at them and bowed. One by one he removed the four pistols and dropped them noisily onto the wood table. His smile disappeared and he looked intently at each of the Dons' faces.

'I don't want you to say a word,' he told them coldly. 'Only know this: Qhe and I cannot be touched. He and I are safe. You don't even know how to begin. It's you – each one of you – who are in danger. Just behave yourselves. Remember. Behave.' He paused to allow time for his words to sink in and then continued: 'I will see you again soon – to cement our relationship.'

He glared at them once more then abruptly left the room.

'Holy Jesus!' the man from New York swore.

'The cat thinks he's superman.'

'Perhaps he is.'

'He makes us look like clumsy midgets.'

'Goddam him!'

'Gentlemen,' Goldino raised his hands to silence his brother Dons, 'I think maybe we've learned to do business with them. And I think maybe we owe an apology to Don Gillamo. My feeling now is that Don Gillamo's discretion in signing them in *was* correct. We must learn how to expand and absorb.'

'You mean it's like making a pact with the goddam devil!'

None of them laughed.

Eight hours later, Willard was back in the International Gems building in Marseilles and going through three files. He wanted to read them alone to absorb their full import and had dismissed the two Pashmani warriors who hovered by his shoulder. They had begun to say something about a problem, but he had told them that he would deal with it later. For the moment he was totally absorbed in the information at hand.

The investigation had been done superbly. The three Prophets had tried to wipe out their past, but history was history and could never be completely eradicated. Willard supressed a slight smile of glee as he read through the pages. The three separate stories were similar and stank.

The European was from Sweden. In his teens he had entered a Franciscan monastery, but had been thrown out for incessant buggery. He had then attempted unsuccessfully to train as a priest in half a dozen other churches. Each failure had been marked by the burning down of a church and he had finally served a three-year prison sentence for arson. After his release, he had set up a bogus psychiatric care unit for ex-prisoners which became nothing more or less than a pimps' employment agency. He had then met a bishop from an obscure church with no more than a dozen followers and bribed his way into holy orders. He opened a chapel of his own near Stockholm which became infamous for rumoured black magic rites and orgies. As a police investigation into it had reached its climax, there had been a series of gruesome murders and the man had disappeared.

The Persian Prophet's story was equally tasty. He, was in fact an Ethiopian Jew. Uneducated and illiterate, he had started work as a tourist guide and hustler in Addis Ababa and had soon progressed to becoming a petty thief and extortionist. At the age of twenty, he had been running a protection racket for all the souvenir shops. His life had changed when he met some rich Libyan tourists and he converted to Islam in order to get a free trip to Mecca on the pilgrimage. He had remained in Mecca for several years, hustling the naïve pilgrims, and at the same time picking up pieces of the Sufi lore of sorcery. He spent the next few years travelling back and forth across North Africa and the Middle East searching out magicians, witches, sorcerers and healers to learn their trade. He had finally fallen in with an occult group in the Iranian capital of Tehran where he achieved sinister notoriety as a purveyor of love and death potions, charms for success and failure, and teller of the future. He had also acquired the technique of mass hypnosis and came into the pay of a rival group to the Shah. He had used his dubious calling to undermine and blackmail, all of which led to an insurrection in which five hundred innocent men and women died. After this, he disappeared too.

The third member of the trio, the man who was the Japanese Prophet, was a psychopathic master of Kung Fu, Tai Chi and Karate. His father had been a fanatic Japanese patriot and believer in the ancient disciplines. At the age of fifteen he had 'accidentally' killed his father in a mock fight and immediately became a hero to a hundred young thugs in Tokyo. He had organized them into chapters to practise the martial arts and terrorize the suburbs of Tokyo. He then spent two years in a juvenile detention centre where he read books on Zen and tantric magic. After his release, he went to live totally alone in the mountains for two years. He reappeared to open a small school teaching the martial arts, but which had a secret core that practised tantric and other forms of sexual magic. Young children in the district had disappeared, and there was a police investigation that discovered nothing definite. The school flourished and he finally decided to stand as a member of parliament. There were minor riots and two of his opponents died mysteriously. However, he did not win the parliamentary seat and that was what pushed him right over the edge. He began claiming openly that he was Japan's greatest sorcerer and that anyone who stood in his way would be cast down by a spell. He attracted thousands of freaks and started his own minor religious movement which involved itself in every kind of dubious occult practice. A few days after his mother appeared in a television interview denouncing her own son and pleading with him, she was found murdered. Then he, too, disappeared.

In each file were police and press photographs of the three men as they had looked in the past. There were also photocopies of the original police records and statements from others who had been involved.

All in all, they were psychic hooligans of the highest order. When the man who called himself the Prophet had chosen them to be his mystical henchmen, he had chosen well. Each of them was ready and more than willing to do anything for the rewards that he promised and already they had gone a long way to fulfilling their devious lust for macabre glory.

With a deep sigh, Willard threw the files down onto the desk and called in the waiting Pashmani warriors.

'Where's the journalist, Purot?' he asked.

'As Qhe suggested, we had to put him temporarily to sleep. He was most unco-operative.'

'Well, you can wake him now,' Willard said with satisfaction. 'I think he'll be only too happy to co-operate. And the girl?'

The three Pashmanis' faces fell.

'She's in the chateau,' one of them finally answered. 'She was captured by the Prophets.'

'And just what,' Willard asked with a grave frown, 'was she doing there?'

'Taking photographs with a telescopic lens. She had darkened her face and coloured her hair, and was dressed in our clothes.'

'Qhe told you to keep her safe,' Willard reprimanded.

'He also told us to treat her as a sister – which we did. We treated her with respect.'

Willard nodded slowly. Now that he had read the truth about the three Prophets, he did not fancy her chances at all – not at all. There was also the added confusion that Don Gillamo and his family thought that Qhe had dealt with her.

'Very well,' Willard said, 'we've got to move fast. Wake the journalist Purot. We're going to publish this stuff,' he pointed at the three files. 'And we're going to publish it soon.'

'And the girl?'

'If she is a sister,' Willard replied sadly, 'then we treat her as one. We are all of us ready to sacrifice.'

The Pashmanis nodded understandingly. They could only wish her luck.

EIGHTEEN

It was a living nightmare. For three days and nights, Qhe had been continuously in the presence of the Prophet. For seventy-two hours he had worshipped, praised and glorified this horrible man. Always in the cavern with its ever-burning fires, day had merged into night and time had become meaningless. Qhe was beginning to lose himself in this maze of evil fantasy and waited impatiently for the Prophet to cease this fanatic rhythm.

For the Prophet all this was a luxury for which he had long waited. He had a companion who truly appreciated all that he was and all that he was doing. With deep understanding and infinite greed for knowledge, this Qhe was absorbing all his wisdom and power. This Qhe seemed to adore his very movements and way of talking. Oh, indeed it was glorious to have a companion who could *see* him, really see him!

Now that he had an appreciative audience, the Prophet was more conceited than ever. His megalomaniac ego was swelling hour by hour and hour by hour he was drawing Qhe closer into a more intimate relationship.

'And yet I have told you hardly anything!' his voice boomed. 'You see only a tenth of the vision. How can I expand your sight to see everything?'

'Master, the little that I see is wonderful enough. More would make me tremble against the earth like the worm that I am before you.'

'Little child, how worthy you are to be at my side. With me you shall watch as I rule the planet. The spirit world already worships at my feet. Humanity has yet to follow.'

'The spirits?' Qhe asked with glowing innocence. 'How do they worship you? Are they all at your command?'

'All of them! All! You can have no idea.'

'But I want to know.'

'You could not stand it. No ordinary mortal could bear it!'

'Let me try,' Qhe pleaded. 'Let that be the test to see if I am truly worthy.'

'You could not bear it,' the Prophet boasted. 'No other man could bear it.'

Qhe pulled back his shoulders and held his head straight. Only occasionally did he let himself appear strong and dignified before the Prophet. It added reality. It made the Prophet ever more enthused by his new devotee.

'You could not bear it,' he repeated.

'Lord, let me try. You know that I am no innocent or weakling. If I am to be your shadow I must know all. And surely if I am not strong enough, you have the power to protect me.'

This did it. This was the bait that the Prophet could not resist. And it was true: if this man was to be his lieutenant, then he had to be initiated into the knowledge. He stood, taking Qhe by the arm. His huge muscled torso made Qhe look a pathetic physical specimen.

'One day,' he told Qhe, 'you will have a body like mine. You will actually look like a god among men.'

Qhe nodded in wonderment, in fact not knowing what to say for the idea of looking like an enormous hunk of beefcake horrified him.

'You know,' the Prophet continued, 'I am actually beginning to develop an affection for you. It is an emotion that is normally alien to me. Not for two hundred years have I...' He looked down at Qhe and smiled mysteriously.

'Did you realize?' he asked.

'I had half-guessed,' Qhe answered nervously.

'That, too, is a magic that I shall teach you. Those pathetic slugs who come to worship me, give themselves to me. They have no idea. You, my little child, are the first man to have ever been able to resist. I applaud you, my little pupil. It shows some force.'

'Then why have you taken so long to commence?' Qhe asked.

'The arts, my child, the arts. These devils and demons

needed years to come under my control. Do you know,' he said, beaming his radiant smile, 'that they are all around. Not a square inch of the air is free of them and they are all – all – pledged to me and to me alone. Come.'

As he led Qhe away down a corridor which Qhe had not previously seen, he clapped his hands and indicated that a dozen of the young boys who had been waiting at the side should follow them. The twelve children ran eagerly forward, maniacal smiles on their faces and their eyes glowing with a strangely sinister look.

'The men you see here with me,' the Prophet told Qhe, 'were once children like these. Not all of them survive. In fact, few of them do. But they serve their purpose magnificently as you will see.'

The corridor was dark and musky. It held an atmosphere of evil that intensified as they moved down it. Three hundred yards along, it ended abruptly. The Prophet looked at the bare rock and roared at it. A concealed door swung open at the correct vibrations in the Prophet's voice.

They now entered yet another chamber which was circular and its floor, walls and ceiling were of black marble. It was lit by torches held in iron brackets.

'This,' the Prophet announced, 'is where I do my real work.'

Qhe nodded eagerly and his eyes traversed the chamber. At the four points of the compass were incense burners filled with glowing charcoal, but as yet with no perfume upon them. At the centre of the chamber was a large circle formed by human skulls and placed in this circle at equal intervals were twelve iron chairs with straps and chains attached to them.

'Throw incense on the burners, my children,' the Prophet ordered.

The twelve young boys, naked as always, darted eagerly across the room to fulfil their master's command. There was now a macabre eagerness about them that was truly eery and Qhe wondered if he could bear the sight of these demented children being so horribly used for much longer. Also in his mind was the idea that at some time, at some inevitable point in the future, he would have to do battle with the Prophet. He only prayed that it would be soon.

The chamber began to fill with the smoke and odour of the incense. It was a scent that made Qhe's throat dry up and his hands become damp and clammy.

'To your seats, children, to your seats!' the Prophet roared.

The boys pranced across the chamber and, with great clangings and rattlings, sat down in the iron chairs. To Qhe, the chairs looked like medieval instruments of torture and he was confused by the apparent eagerness of the children to be in them. They were like kids at Christmas with their first electric train set. He did not even want to stretch his mind to what they would be used for, but *God preserve me from callousness*, he silently prayed.

'Help me strap and chain them in,' the Prophet ordered Qhe, 'and make certain they're secure, absolutely secure.'

Qhe moved to lock the first boy into his chair.

'Tighter, they must be tighter,' the seven-year-old whispered vehemently.

Qhe suppressed a look of disgust and pain as he pulled the chains to dig deep into the boy's arms and thighs.

'That's good, that's good,' the child whispered, 'I cannot move.'

Qhe continued helping with this gruesome work feeling increasingly sick at the scene and at himself. He longed to do battle with the Prophet this very moment, but knew that that alone would not destroy the man's gargantuan operation.

'Are you ready now?' the Prophet roared.

Qhe managed to maintain his look of innocent enthusiasm tinged with a greed for magical knowledge as he nodded to the Prophet.

'Then come here! Come and watch the might of my power.'

Qhe stood beside him at the centre of the evil circle, surrounded by the vacant skulls and the ghastly looks of frenzied anticipation on the boys' faces.

'Be still and be quiet,' the Prophet ordered Qhe. 'Do not

move, do not twitch, do nothing. We shall see.'

Qhe now stood a silent spectator to this pantomine of the devil's work.

'Lohoi! Lahai!' The Prophet roared the same incantation twice.

Directly opposite them, twenty feet above the ground, a concealed slab of rock slid open. It revealed a wedge-shaped vent that gave a full view of the huge black cube that stood in the mammoth hollow in the desert and which was the focal point for all the forces and energies. There was an immediate triple action. Light flooded into the chamber from outside. At the same time, it seemed as if all the air from the chamber was sucked out. Qhe felt his chest cave in and collapse as he watched the incense smoke streaming up through the vent. Only a few seconds later, air came rushing back in with a hissing noise, bellowing up Qhe's lungs. The atmosphere shimmered and flickered with strange lights and shapes.

His feet held firmly apart, his stance that of the supreme warrior, the Prophet looked authoritatively up at the cube. He glanced quickly at Qhe to see his reaction and Qhe looked back at him, his expression wondrous and awed. The Prophet nodded with satisfaction.

'Maion! Lando! Trynos! Lavanteen! Hail! Hail! Hail! Xul! Tferd! Leira! Zad! Hail! Hail! Hail! Wilmuss! Zeneroid! Paltron! Yanaeus! Hail! Hail! Hail!'

The Prophet roared each call with a different intonation and vibration. At each one, the air shimmered and moved and the chained children shivered and twitched. The atmosphere was unbelievably dense. Qhe was silently and continuously repeating to himself *with light, with love, with power* to keep himself centred, conscious, calm – and safe.

The Prophet stood majestically with his left arm pointed at the ground and his right arm pointed towards the ceiling. His three middle fingers were extended in demonic greeting. His eyes rolled down to the earth, then up to the ceiling, and he breathed in a huge amount of air. He held it in the top of his lungs, then lowered it down his chest and into his stomach. His stomach muscles strained and rippled as they compressed the air until he raised it back up into his chest and exhaled it directly at one of the children. Instantly, the boy fell unconscious. He repeated this action eleven times until all the children had been put under. Then once again, he repeated his calls:

'Maion! Lando! Trynos! Lavanteen! Hail! Hail Hail!'

He went through all twelve calls and, having ended them, let out a deep unholy moan that reverberated around the chamber. The ground began to tremble and the walls and ceiling shake. The mammoth black cube seemed to pulsate and throb. Then the black marble began to change colour, becoming greyer and lighter. The echo from the Prophet's unholy moan continued insistently as if filled with a life of its own. Everything was shaking and moving, and Qhe had to change his stance to keep his balance. Looking down at the ground made him dizzy for even the earth seemed insubstantial. He looked away to the walls, but they were now translucent – in fact, they did not seem to exist. The ceiling was also becoming opaque and disappearing. It was as if the chamber did not exist at all. It had no dimensions, no place, no space.

To Qhe, it looked as though they were floating in air, but an air that was void and without the quality of life. Everything material had gone. He could only see the circle of gleaming skulls and grinning boys' faces, and the huge black cube. The cube itself was expanding. Wherever Qhe looked it was there. He was outside it, then inside it. It pervaded everything. It appeared to be the whole cosmos. His mind screamed and grated at the visions.

The skulls were dancing and winking. The children's faces were distorting. He looked at one child. For a moment his expression seemed full of bliss and then he began to smile. The smile cracked the features of his face like shattered crystal. Blood poured from the eyes. The smile widened, the mouth expanding to fill the whole face. His head was tearing in two. His flesh became a pulpy mess and he was thrashing wildly. An eye fell from its socket and disappeared from view. His ears hung loose like wet tissue.

It was another face. He was a different person. No, not a person. Some horrible being invoked from the depths of evil to possess his body. An image of such disgusting horror that no man could see it and forget.

The iron chair with its straps and chains disappeared. It was now a sinister throne with this hideous demon squatting upon it, leering and twitching.

Qhe grimaced and looked away, but werever he turned his eyes, the picture was similarly horrifying. Every child had disappeared, his flesh and protoplasm lent for the manifestation of these distorted spirits. Each one was more horrible than the next, each one a worse caricature of disgusting evil.

'I rule thee!' the Prophet roared, sweeping around with his arms outstretched in a sign of power and dominion over them.

'Bow!' he bellowed.

Their distorted skulls cringed forward in obedience to him.

'Work thy plans,' one of the demons rasped hideously. 'Satan himself bows to thee.'

'Thy plans.'

'Thy plans.'

'Satan.'

'Satan.'

The twelve of them sang their discordant symphony at him, their voices rasping, squeaking and echoing.

The Prophet smiled and then roared with laughter.

'Silence, I order thee,' he shouted.

With horrible gurgling and rattling noises they fell quiet, and the Prophet stepped forward. He held forth his hand to one of the disgusting creatures and the beast kissed it. Qhe shuddered at the sight of the touch, but the Prophet turned to him:

'Prove thyself. Prove thyself worthy.'

Qhe's stomach convulsed in revulsion, but he stepped forward. Suddenly he felt a surge of overhwelming anger and fury. Let these beasts touch my hand! his mind screamed. Let there be God's blessing in my flesh for them.

Let them receive the grace of love and light. They cannot touch me!

He held forth his hand and the demon shuddered and pulled away. This only made the Prophet roar with even greater laughter.

'Kiss it!' he commanded.

Qhe felt a horrible shiver grating up his spine as the slimy warm drooling lips brushed across the skin of his hand. Then, following the Prophet, each of the beasts kissed.

The Prophet took Qhe by the shoulders and hugged him to his breast.

'My son, my son and follower.'

He led Qhe back to the centre of the circle. Then, raising his arms, he chanted the words of dismissal and the end of the ceremony.

'Iyao laurandum!'

There was a thundering noise, the ground trembled and shook. For a second everything went black and then the chamber was normal once again. The only sign that anything had happened was the sweating tortured faces of the children.

'Now are you trusted!' the Prophet told Qhe.

Qhe blinked. For a moment the herculean man had disappeared and once more the Prophet seemed only an aged and withered man. He blinked again and the Prophet was himself.

'Lord, I need sleep,' Qhe said with infinite weariness. 'I must sleep.'

NINETEEN

Huddled in a corner of the chamber that held the sorcerer's equipment, Qhe desperately tried to calm himself, to rediscover himself and to rediscover the light within. He had tried to sleep, but his brain was racing on that which he had just seen and that in which he had just participated.

May God forgive me. May God forgive me, he whispered to himself. He could still feel the touch of the demons on his flesh, but it was the approval of the Prophet that most disgusted him. Every part of him was revolted by all that happened and he could feel himself losing sight of why he was truly there. It was almost impossible for him to imagine that an outside world existed, a world of ordinary people and of light. He could feel a rare streak of callousness rising in his consciousness. Let the Prophet rule the world. Let him fulfil his greed. Only let me have peace.

He looked around the chamber at the gruesome bottles and jars containing their dead animals and insects. His eye fixed on the corpse of a tiny sparrow. It lay on its side, its face pathetic and its body completely vulnerable. Little bird, little bird, Qhe thought. Once you flew free in the skies. Once you sang and built your nest. You joined the dawn chorus and swooped in the rays of the sun. And now? And now . . .

Qhe smiled at his sentimentality, but the sparrow was a symbol for all that was pathetic and sad. His eyes reddened, and a tear rolled down his cheek. He smiled again as the tear reached his mouth and he tasted its saltiness. Well, at least he was still human. At least, he could still cry. At least . . . Suddenly he saw himself clearly sitting there, cringing and pathetic. Good God, what sort of a man was he? Had he forgotten everything? Had he lost his power and vision? Had he forgotten that he was there by his own choice? Had he forgotten that there was work to do?

He viciously slapped his face and then stood up. He had seen the Prophet. He had him eating out of his hand. Everything was running perfectly. He knew that the Prophet's herculean body housed only a warped and evil old man whose sorcery was like an ever-increasing snowball But snow melted in the heat. Winter was always followed by Spring. This place was not the whole of the world? It was a warped pocket of energy that would be destroyed. He would destroy it.

Mentally he pieced the jigsaw together: Gillamo and his family, the three Prophets, the money, the conference in two weeks – and the Prophet. Qhe now sat crosslegged and began to breathe gently and rhythmically. He imagined that there was a huge funnel that connected him with the sky miles above and that down this tunnel poured pure vibrational energy. He drew it into his lungs, absorbed it into his chest and then passed it around his body. He imagined this clean vibrational force permeating every atom of his blood, fat and muscle. He then willed the energy to cleanse and refortify his ethereal, astral and mental bodies. For over half an hour he did nothing else.

Now, once again, he turned his mind to the Prophet. Soon, perhaps even now, the three Prophets were being exposed in the press. Qhe refused to allow the idea that his warriors had found out nothing about them surface in his consciousness. Willard had Don Gillamo and the other Dons under control. It was obvious what Qhe had to do next, but after that, what then? For a second he began to panic. He suddenly saw that no matter how successfully he destroyed the physical form of the Prophet and his work, it would still exist on the astral and mental planes. It would still exist to push men's minds into malevolent greed and prevent world peace. The conference would fail and there would always be a permanent blob of sucking evil polluting the psychic atmosphere of the planet.

There seemed to be no answer, no solution in which to dissolve the Prophet's carefully worked magic. Qhe could dismantle the Prophet's framework and crush the black astral cube, but how then to absorb its astral energies? He would have to find men who were prepared to absorb the energies into themselves and then, with prayer and yoga, transmute it into a harmless atmosphere. But how many men on the planet were capable of such high magical work? A hundred? Perhaps less. And how many years would it take them? And for that time, the blob of energy would float around attracted by any person's or organization's thoughts reinforcing them.

Qhe felt his stomach tighten and a bead of sweat begin to run down his forehead. He was pathetic. It was useless! He looked round the chamber and a cold feeling of total futility filled his body and mind. Just as suddenly, a voice in the back of his mind told him, *ordered* him to put himself immediately into a meditative state.

Again, he viciously slapped his face. He sat crosslegged and focused on the sad corpse of the tiny sparrow. He used the dead bird as a centering device to still his mind and quieten his emotions. He breathed slowly and rhythmically, once more creating a funnel of energy up into the clear sky miles above. *Qhe, dear sweet Qhe,* he heard a voice echoing within him. He smiled at the game he was playing with himself. *Be calm, dear boy, be calm.* Qhe's smile deepened as he heard the comforting words of his own subconscious mind. *No, no, I am not your mind. I am separate.* Qhe's smile turned to a frown as he realized that it was the spirits playing games with him. Be gone, he ordered authoritatively. *Neither am I a spirit, dear boy. You know me.*

Qhe breathed in more deeply and repeated a Sanskrit mantra in order to silence his mind totally and dismiss anything around him. But the voice came back again: *raise your energies higher.* No spirit would have told him to do this and there was a warmth and strength in the voice's vibration that was certainly not his own. He willed to focus his consciousness at the very top and back of his head. His mind went quiet. There were no images across his eyes, only the shimmering blackness of spirit.

Out of this blackness a single tiny point of light appeared, getting slowly larger and coming closer. Within it there was an image of a face, a face that was distantly familiar and that held a look of infinite compassion and understanding. Qhe mentally bowed before him and apologised for daring to insult him.

No matter, my boy, no matter, came the answer. *I said that I would watch over you, but that I could not interfere. I come only to advise and suggest. Your work goes brilliantly. Do not be depressed or concerned, and know that you will find a solution. Remember that in the past all things could be made correct by a burning sacrifice to the Gods. The fire of sacrifice can right a thousand wrongs. Only sacrifice that which is most dear. No more. I bless you. Smile for me.*

The point of light receded, carrying the loving image with it and Qhe remained sitting for another thirty minutes. Just seeing that man, that godling, had brought him such a flood of renewed strength and faith that he was shamed by his recent thoughts. But the riddle of the sacrifice ... to sacrifice that which was most dear. Qhe was prepared to sacrifice anything, but what? Then a vision began to dawn upon him and a gentle smile crossed his lips. That would do it! Yes, that would certainly do it! And it would not be easy.

It was time to work again.

Putting the look of devoted adoration back on his face, Qhe walked towards the Prophet's cavern. As he stood at the top of the steps that looked across the stalactites, stalagmites and burning fires, he could sense immediately that something had changed. He narrowed his eyes to focus on the Prophet who was no longer wearing his radiant smile, but grimacing horribly while some men and boys cringed on the ground around him. Qhe could guess what had happened and the timing could not have been more perfect.

'Master, master, all adoration to you, Oh holy one,' Qhe cried as he ran down the steps and across the cavern. 'Thou art glorious and magnificent, wonderful and beauteous. The sun of our day. The moon of our night.'

Qhe continued his chant right up until the very moment he was only ten feet from the Prophet. He ignored the man's glare of fury as if it did not exist, but in the back of his mind Qhe wondered whether some of it would be unleashed upon him. He fell to his knees and looked lovingly up at the Prophet. The Prophet looked back coldly, but Qhe ignored these bad energies and continued looking devotedly up at him. The Prophet could not resist this adoration and melted sufficiently to smile at Qhe.

'My son, my apprentice,' he boomed at Qhe, 'the world is filled with foolish worms. You have no idea what –'

'Master, master,' Qhe interrupted, burbling like an uncontrollably enthusiastic child, 'I have had a dream, a glorious dream. It is the affirmation of all that I have been thinking about you. The world is ready for you! The planet awaits you! The people need you! The energies, the stars, the season – everything is right. They need you to adore and worship! You must not fail their call.'

But the Prophet hardly heard the words so engrossed was he in that which had enraged him.

'Be silent!' he roared.

'I cannot,' Qhe shouted back. 'It is all too glorious. I have seen it clearly. It is already written in the stories of the gods. You shall walk the earth and all shall fall at your feet. They call you now. They call you now!'

'Silence!' he roared again. 'My plans have been put awry! There has been interference, gross interference! I shall wreak my revenge! Look!'

He threw at Qhe copies of English, German, French and American newspapers. Qhe picked them up and each one carried the same front page headline story: the three Prophets of the Prophet had been exposed. There were photographs of them as young men and detailed biographies. No police charges had been made, but deportation orders were being prepared. Qhe tossed the newspapers aside as if they meant nothing.

'So?' Qhe looked up. 'What did you expect?'

'So!' the Prophet shouted with all his might. 'So! So! What did I expect? You snivelling idiot!'

'What did you expect,' Qhe continued, 'from psychic cretins who have no understanding of your true magnifience? Their vision could only go as far as greed. What do you expect from gangsters and criminals? Did it never occur to you that they would make this move? Did it never occur to you that your three Prophets would be blind and ignorant, impotent to this sort of work? Don't you see that it's perfect? They don't realize that their timing is perfect. Everything is ready for you.'

'The Dons did this?' the Prophet asked. 'But they are purely men of greed and stupidity – this is how I could trust them.'

'Yes, they did it. Who else?' Qhe answered. 'And your three apes are powerless. They could not control them. It is glorious!'

'Glorious! How is it glorious?'

'Because the world waits for you, is ready for you, calls for you. You do not realize your magnificence. You do not realize the perfectness of your wonderful fate. How long can you remain hidden here and holding back your wonderful blessing from the people of our planet. It is not fair. It is not just. It is not correct. They need you. They want you. It is written clearly in the stars of providence and fate!'

There was now a sudden silence while the Prophet absorbed what Qhe had said. He looked down at the Pashmani monarch whom he had accepted as his apprentice and remembered that for years he had waited for a servant such as this. Nothing happened by chance. The spirits had brought this man to him. He was more than an omen. He was a reminder of the Prophet's true position and standing. The spirits had sent him as their messenger. He, the Prophet, had been too modest. He was too humble and had not realized the call of humanity for him.

Yes! Qhe was right. What more could he expect from pathetic criminals? What more could he expect from third-class sorcerers?

'And now, my messenger? What now, my messenger?' he asked.

'Oh,' Qhe sighed blissfully, 'the gods sent me to serve you and now I may serve you. This is the most glorious day in my life. Master, master, how wonderful it is. What fools they are,' he said pointing at the newspapers. 'They have no idea what they shall miss. The world awaits you with such longing. Your time of waiting, sweet god, is over.'

'Yes and I have waited long,' the Prophet answered meditatively. 'The work has been hard.'

'But the people call you and all shall be repaid. With your power and your money, everything is yours. Not just their bodies, but their longings, their very souls desire you!'

'And how shall I return?'

'In glory. In wondrous glory. Fate has chosen me to serve you and I shall prepare everything. I have been sent so that your great mind need not even deign to think of details. I am your left hand, and your left eye, your shadow, a mere particle of your consciousness. There are only two things you must do immediately and the rest will be my loving duty to you.'

'And what are those two things?'

'First, you have to withdraw your thread of energy and force from those three hyenas who are your so-called Prophets. They are worthless now, but if they still have access to your powers . . .'

'Of course. I shall break the spell immediately.'

'Secondly, you must sign over management of your money to me. My little finger knows more than all the Dons put together how best to handle it for your purposes. You must remember my other life.'

'Naturally.' The Prophet beamed his smile. Second by second, his thanks to the spirit world increased for sending him this man. 'And then?'

'Let me go to Europe and prepare your way. Your entry shall be such that the world has never seen. Oh the glory of it, the glory of it!'

'And you shall stand at my side,' the Prophet said magnificently.

'I could not,' Qhe blushed and looked away.

'Little child, little apprentice, you shall share my joys and power.'

Qhe bowed and knelt to kiss the Prophet's feet, apparently overwhelmed by this demonic being's generosity.

TWENTY

Marie de Baldeau was frightened and yet at the same time there was a reality in the situation that thrilled her. The anger of the three Prophets at her intrusion with her cameras and the fact that she was supposed to be dead had almost pushed them into killing her immediately. They had not because they found it amusing to toy with her like a cat dangling a mouse from its mouth, but she knew that very shortly the newspapers would publish their exposé and then she would certainly be dead.

Before she had always been frightened by death and pain, but she had taken up the Pashmanis' philosophy of life and magic like a duck takes to water. This was her only sadness: that she would die before she could start her real search for the truth. Her mind was full of a thousand different things. Especially she wondered what she had been in her previous incarnations. Perhaps she had been a Pashmani warrior or a Tibetan priest for she was certainly no stranger to magic. She had a natural aptitude for it that could only have come from the work of previous lifetimes. She could feel the energies of her body as clearly as she could see her little finger and she was amazed at their power – both for good and for bad.

Well, if she was to die, she would die nobly and not whimpering. She felt only disgust for the Three Prophets and even if they tortured her, she knew that would end in the release of death. *With light, with love, with power*. Such simple words, but they rang a bell of glorious truth in her. Why weren't they taught in schools, she wondered? Why didn't my parents tell me these things? The world was upside down. If she could have started her life all over again, she would have gone to Pashman and asked Qhe to be her teacher. *Qhe*, she sighed, how I would have loved you to be my teacher and older brother. She would just have to wait for her next incarnation – maybe then she would be a man and Qhe a woman. She laughed to herself and, as she did so, the door to her tiny room swung open.

'You have little time left to laugh,' sneered one of the Prophets' robed attendants.

She continued smiling and he slapped her hard across the face, sending her flying against the wall. He looked down at her shaking body and laughed. He then placed his foot on her neck and held her rigid.

'I could kill you now,' he told her, 'but they have other plans for you. They are angry, angrier than I have ever seen – and their fury is directed against you.'

He brutally lifted her from the floor and threw her into the arms of a second man who twisted her round and sent her hurtling down the corridor. A third attendant snorted with amusement and rubbed the sole of his shoe against the skin of her face. Then they shoved and kicked her along the floor into the main hall.

She was not clairvoyant, but it would have taken a mindless block of stone not to feel the volcanic red and black colours that filled the auras of the three Prophets.

'Yesterday,' said the Japanese.

'Yesterday,' repeated the European.

'Yesterday,' said the Persian.

'All my troubles seemed so far away,' Marie sang back.

They fixed her with a look of such evil intensity that immediately her body felt stiff and cold.

The Japanese held up a headline from the English *Daily Mirror* that read *Prophets in it for Profits*. The centre of the paper carried police photographs of each of the three men.

'You did this,' the Persian said.

'And for it you will suffer,' added the European.

'Does it matter where we come from or who we were?' screamed the Japanese. 'We are *his* Prophets. We carry *his* power. We are the forerunners of *his* glory.'

'Your pathetic vision,' shrieked the European, 'does not see into the truth. You meddle. You interfere. You clash with energies.'

'And now you will really feel them!'

'You are a worm!'
'A slug!'
'A termite!'
'Pathetic!'
'Feeble!'
'Weak!'

They spat each word with such venomous energy that she recoiled shuddering as they spoke. Her body trembled with fear and she tried to control it. She would not appear frightened, but her skin shivered uncontrollably. She tried again to calm herself, but could not, and, because of this, she felt a sudden wave of anger surging through her.

Her mind rejected their spiteful words. She imagined that they were shouting at themselves and not at her.

'Blasphemers,' she hissed at them. 'Children of the Devil. Offspring of demons. Demented tortured unknowing minds from the past. You know nothing of true glory! You know nothing of true greatness! Your vision is seen from beneath a slimy rock! You are lost souls! Only light and love can save you!'

Her voice became louder and louder. At the same time the three Prophets increased the hissed venom of their own words. The force generated in this bizarre psychic battle was so powerful that the watching attendants were thrown back against the walls of the hall to watch and listen, their mouths hanging open. They had never seen anyone before who could resist the three Prophets' energy, moreover the Prophets, too, were bewildered and panicked by her force.

Marie felt herself becoming increasingly strong second by second. It was as if she had plugged herself into some unknown source of power that she was just allowing to flow through her. Her courage and faith had locked her into an infinite reservoir of light and strength, as it does for any man who truly trusts to faith. Let them kill me, her mind said clearly to herself while she continued telling them that they were children of darkness and that they should see the light. Let them kill me! It matters not. I am a warrior for light and love!

Her shouting and their hysterical magical screaming

reached a deafening crescendo. Then, just for a moment, the three Prophets paused.

'May God bless you,' she chanted at them.

'No!' they shouted back in unison and shuddered.

'May God bless you,' she repeated.

'Never!' they screamed. 'We call down *his* energy upon you. We call down the force of the Prophet against you. He will avenge. He will destroy.'

The three Prophets raised their arms in the air and sounded out the psychic vibration to tune into the Prophet and the power of his astral cube in the Sahara.

Nothing happened.

Marie stood calmly there, smiling at them.

'God bless you,' she repeated over and over again.

Each time she said it now, they recoiled as if lashed by a bull-whip. In total panic, they looked to each other for an answer. Without a shadow of a doubt, they knew that *he* had withdrawn his force from them. They no longer had the power. They could only rely upon themselves. They had depended upon his energy for so many years now that they felt like beached fishes madly flapping on the sand.

Their faces now just looked mean and twisted. If their magical forces could not destroy this girl, then brute force would. They leapt forward, but she raised her hands hurling white energy at them and they stopped as if they had run into a brick wall.

'Very beautiful, mademoiselle,' she heard a familiar voice saying behind her. 'I am glad to see that you do not need us.'

She turned to see Qhe's smiling face and, with him, three of his warriors. She, too, smiled and then the effort of continuing to hold the energy was too great. Her eyes opened wide, she made a slight whistling noise and then wilted like a flower. The second that she fell, the three Prophets sprang forward only to meet three pairs of strong Pashmani hands. Gripped by their neck nerves, they felt instant pain and a few seconds later felt nothing as they fell unconscious to the floor.

*

As the long-base white convertible Rolls-Royce sped along the highway from Grenoble to Marseilles, Qhe put a call on the car's phone through to his private number in Marseilles.

'How do you do, sweetheart?' Qhe asked Willard who answered the phone.

'You're a bit late, aren't you, old fruit?' Willard replied.

'I thought I'd go to the chateau and see about young Marie.'

'Did you get her out? How is she?' Willard asked.

'Fine. Sleeping like a babe in the car at the moment. She didn't need our help.'

'Well, maybe we need hers,' Willard replied. 'Gillamo's gone totally loopy since the exposés were published. The other Dons went back to America, leaving Goldino who's their top money man here as another set of eyes. They made it clear that if anything went wrong, Gillamo would swing for it. They also put the bulk of their money in with the Movement's.'

'What's he done then?'

'He's bought off the Marseilles force for a couple of days and he's got a hundred men surrounding the building here – maybe more. Naturally, I don't fancy his chances, but it's all rather messy, isn't it? Gillamo thinks the entire Mafia is threatened. Incidentally, how's the Prophet?'

'About to crawl out of his shell,' Qhe answered, laughing at his friend's English phlegmatism.

'Can you do something to calm Gillamo and Goldino?'

'Yes, I think so.'

'Well, get a move on. I've a feeling the idiots are about to start. Toodle-oo.'

Qhe put down the phone and chuckled. His smile suddenly turned to a frown.

'Put your foot down,' he ordered the Pashmani driver.

The warrior nodded and pressed down the accelerator. An hour later, having cruised at a steady one hundred and twenty-five miles per hour, they approached the suburbs of Marseilles.

A mile into the town and they could hear the sound of gunfire. Next they saw a huge crowd being held back

by police barriers. The whole area for a quarter of a mil
around the International Gems building had been cord
oned off.

'Take the car through the crowd!' Qhe commande
urgently.

The horn blaring continuously, the Rolls inched its wa
through the people until it reached the barrier where a half
dozen gendarmes blocked their way.

'No entry, Monsieur, onto the film set. Turn aroun
immediately. They are shooting a very important film -
very important.'

Qhe stood up in the back of the car and his face showe
nothing but total rage.

'Film?' he roared. 'An important film. You dare to tel
me they are making an important film!'

The policeman looked totally perplexed and shrugged.

'I,' Qhe continued screaming, 'am that film's produce
and you dare to block my way! I even have the star wit
me!'

He kicked Marie's sleeping body and she sat bolt upright

'Smile,' Qhe hissed at her, 'throw a kiss at the police.'

Marie had just woken from a peaceful dream. Was she i
another dream? she asked herself, but she smiled and ble
the policeman a kiss.

'Remove the barrier!' Qhe shouted authoritatively. 'W
are already late.'

The policeman looked at the angry foreign gentleman
the brilliant white Rolls-Royce, the chauffeur and atten
dants, and the beautiful girl dressed so peculiarly in viole
– naturally, she was the star.

'Open it, you fools!' the gendarme ordered his colleague
and stood back apologetically to salute the celluloid mogu
and his star.

The car slid smoothly away onto the 'film set' and th
sound of gunfire grew louder.

'Is this a film?' Marie asked, confused.

'Guess,' Qhe answered.

Coming round a corner, a man with a sub-machine gu
barred their way. He let off a two second volley before hi

body was bounced off the bonnet of the Rolls and against a wall.

'Some film!' Marie exclaimed. 'Just what the hell is ...'

But she was cut short by the sound of a man talking through a loudhailer.

'We have the men and we have the guns,' the voice echoed down the street. 'You've seen them and heard them. Come out now and you won't be hurt. We'll give you two minutes to make your decision and then we'll come in to get you.'

There was another round of firing and then silence.

'Slowly,' Qhe told his driver. 'Very slowly until I tell you.'

The faces of householders who had been ordered by the police to stay inside while the filming took place peeked out from behind blinds and curtains. Qhe looked up and smiled reassuringly at them, but the atmosphere was very eery. This section of the city normally throbbed with cosmopolitan life and there was now a tense quiet hanging over it, broken only buy the purring noise of the Rolls' engine.

'Even more slowly,' Qhe whispered as they approached the corner that opened onto the road that passed in front of his building.

The sleek bonnet edged its way gently round. A few feet away a dozen men spun round – they were carrying machine-guns, high-powered rifles and anti-tank bazookas. Beyond them stood another group of men, similarly armed, and past them a man stood with a portable loudspeaker beside an armoured jeep. All along the road, men were waiting anxiously in doorways for the order to move.

The dozen men closest to the car raised their weapons.

'Move!' Qhe shouted.

The driver's foot hit the gas pedal and the car leaped forward, carving a path through the men. All hell was let loose as a hundred tense gangsters turned to deal with this attack from the rear.

'Down! All down!' Qhe ordered as a shower of bullets struck the sides of the vehicle. 'Brake!'

The car skidded abruptly to a screeching halt as bullets

continued thwacking and ricocheting off the bodywork. Qhe then dove from the car, grabbing the megaphone from the man and somersaulting to protection under the armoured jeep.

'We have no weapons!' he screamed through the loudhailer. 'Call off your monkeys, Gillamo! You've gone crazy. You're going to miss out on a hit bigger than anything you've ever dreamed of. Call them off!'

The shower of bullets continued for a few seconds and then Gillamo's voice could be heard over another loudspeaker ordering his men to cease fire.

'What story you got this time, Qhe? You've done nothing but screw up this deal from beginning to end.'

'I've done nothing, but set it up for us,' Qhe hailed back. 'You think I make a profession of cutting my own throat? Nothing else would bring the Prophet out from his cover, goddammit! Even with your peanut brain you can see that! Don't you see what will come flowing in when he's actually here? Use your warped imagination.'

Hidden in a room overlooking the street, Gillamo turned to his fellow Don, Goldino.

'I want to kill him now and get it over with,' he hissed.

'Sure, sure,' Goldino agreed, thoughtfully cleaning his thick-lensed spectacles. 'But...'

'But what? But nothing. We should rub him out here and now and forget the whole business! I don't know what his game is, but it's screwing up everything. We should just get out of this whole business – take revenge and get out.'

'Yes, yes,' Goldino agreed again, 'but this isn't the twenties and he has a point.'

'A point? What point?'

'Why should he want to cut his own throat?'

'He's a looloo – that's why.'

'He's not,' Goldino answered slowly. 'If I know anything, he's shrewd, one of the shrewdest. This cat's known what he's been doing from the beginning. And if the Prophet does come out into the open ... You know, Gillamo, the family's always wanted to control a religion...'

'Kill him! Kill him now, that's what I say.'

'No, we can always do that later. I think maybe he's right – that we're crazy, that we're going to miss out on the biggest score this planet has ever seen. Huh?'

Gillamo looked brutally at Goldino, but this was no real fight. Goldino was the voice for all the other Dons and the family had always been a democracy – agree or get out. He nodded.

'Put your hands up and stand,' he shouted through the megaphone. 'And everyone else in the car.'

Qhe slowly pulled himself out from under the jeep and lifted his arms in the air. His three warriors and Marie climbed out of the Rolls doing the same. Four of Gillamo's men immediately rushed forward to hold Qhe.

'Nobody,' Qhe whispered at them, 'nobody touches me!'

His words were spoken quietly, but with such dynamic forcefulness that the four men stopped dead. One of them, a huge gorilla of a man, sweat pouring down his face, nervously fingered the trigger of his gun.

'Nobody, buddy?' he said. 'I ain't nobody.'

His face held a vicious leer as he approached Qhe.

'Nobody!' Qhe repeated and looked deep into the man's eyes.

The gorilla stopped dead again, rooted immobile to the spot, and Qhe gently removed the gun from his hand which he then hurled away.

Another group of Gillamo's men had approached to look after the warriors and Marie.

'Hi, toots,' one of them said. 'I know what we're doing tonight.'

Marie spun around.

'Oh, I like a broad with guts,' the man continued and moved forward to touch her.

Instantaneously, the three warriors and Marie shot him a look of such power that his machine-gun dropped to the ground as he clasped at his forehead to soothe the pain. Another man now stepped towards them and he too suddenly felt the most terrible headache.

'Call your men off properly, Gillamo,' Qhe shouted, 'unless you want to open a clinic for them.'

Gillamo, with Goldino at his side, now appeared in the street and Qhe gave them both a look of such affection that they both smiled.

'You've no idea,' Qhe said to them, 'how silly it would have been to kill us. You've no idea what you would have missed.'

TWENTY-ONE

Boy oh boy. Boy oh boy oh boy, was the main thought running through Gillamo's mind as he watched the frenzied activity in the International Gems building.

'What a hot number!' he exclaimed to Don Goldino. 'This Prophet sure is some burning potato! There's never been a show like this. The family's going to be proud, real proud.'

Even Goldino, normally worried and calculating, could not suppress a grin.

'It beats running the numbers racket on lower East-side, that's for certain,' he joked. 'And its nice timing. The day we have the rally – I mean the Second Coming – we'll also put the screws on the British Government. They give in or they lose control of their currency. All in all it will be a day to remember. Just look at it.'

A smile of deep satisfaction on both their faces, they looked round the open plan office. The atmosphere resembled that of a political headquarters the day before an election – a frenzy of activity and expectation.

Posters were being stuck up all over Europe. Radio spots had been booked on all the international commercial radic stations. Press advertizing and public relations were being executed worldwide. Chartered planes were being organized to bring in the pilgrims. Every single international airline was adjusting its schedules to bring people to the South of France for the rally. Every name and address listed in the files of the Prophets of the Prophet movement was being contacted and informed of *his* coming. The switchboard in the building was continuously jammed with calls for information. Hippies and religious and occult freaks of every description were already hitch-hiking their way down to the Mediterranean from all parts of Europe and some were even returning from their pilgrimages to Nepal and northern India. The Salvation Army was sending a brass-band; the Hare Krishna were coming with food to give away; the Jesus movements were arriving with banners; Sufis were driving down with whirling dervish groups. Everyone was coming, because no one wanted to chance missing what might be the Second Coming.

Astrologers were predicting the day of the rally would be the true day of the dawning of the Age of Aquarius. The Plymouth Brethren, the Children of God and the Scientologists were all taking to the hills, loudly moaning the imminent arrival of another global flood.

Willard was masterminding the propaganda like an army general. He had started by saying that the Prophet himself had ordered the exposing of his three Prophets because, once he had learned the truth about their past, he could not condone such evil behaviour. Now *he* was coming himself and he asked people to come – not to worship him, but with open minds to seek the truth. He demanded nothing of his followers, neither devotion or money. He was coming to love them, not to have them love *him*. It was a message that was infinitely appealing – and it was working, truly working.

'You know what we've forgotten?' Gillamo asked Goldino.

'What?'

'All the punks around here who don't owe us a favour yet. We've got to give them the ice-cream and hotdog franchises for the show. They'll make more money in a day than they do the whole of the season.'

'You don't forget anything, do you?' Goldino answered sarcastically, but then he smiled as Willard and Marie approached. 'Do you have permission from the French Government for the venue yet?'

'Yes,' Willard answered friendly. 'They've agreed to that area in the hills behind Antibes. They couldn't really refuse – there are already about fifteen thousand people camping there and waiting.'

'It's good, very good. But, listen, you and I had better get our heads together soon to work out the way we're going to move the money after this shebang is over. That, you will remember, is the real work.'

Goldino's eyes glistened as he thought of the vast sums of money at their disposal – enough to destroy any currency, enough to buy a South American or African country. Enough for anything! Since childhood this had been fantasy and now it was being fulfilled. He was a physical weakling, but he had a mind that knew money, dreamed money, lived money. Pleasure, women, they meant nothing to him. For him the only sexual satisfaction came from financial power, from seeing the globe as one huge Monopoly game with him throwing the dice – for every turn. He thanked God that he had been born into the Mafia – where else would he have had such opportunity to fulfil his warped fantasies.

'Yes, that *is* the real work,' Willard agreed. 'Money – money, money, money.'

'And that International Monetary Conference in Nairobi, well –' Goldino smiled nastily '– it will just go up in smoke.'

'It will indeed,' Willard replied wryly. 'Right up in smoke.'

Then, laughing, he slapped Gillamo and Goldino on the back.

'A beautiful life, what?' he said.

'Yeah, beautiful!' Goldino rasped.

Gillamo's face suddenly dropped as if he had seen a ghost. His lips tightened and he looked quizzically at his brother Don and Willard.

'But supposing,' he said, 'the Prophet cat doesn't show?'

'It does not affect our control of the money,' Goldino answered calculatingly. 'We'll just have less to play with. We won't own a religion – that's all.'

'He'll be here all right,' Willard also replied. 'Don't worry about that. Qhe's with him now.'

'And . . . well . . .' Gillamo was still worrying. 'Supposing he doesn't please the audience? We'll have an angry mob on our hands – millions of them.'

'He'll please them,' Willard winked. 'You can bet your last dollar on that.'

*

Seven hundred and fifty miles away, dressed in his own immaculate pinstripe suit, Qhe was entering the president's office of one of the five big banks in Zurich, Switzerland. He was carrying an executive briefcase with the Pashmani royal seal of the seven-pointed star beneath the sign of infinity embossed in gold over the lock.

The president of the bank, a small man in a dark suit and with a dark banker's expression, greeted Qhe deferentially.

'Your Majesty,' he said. 'It is an honour to see you here. It is – what? – seven years or more since we last met.'

Qhe nodded and, smiling, shook the man's hand.

There was a silence as a tail-coated valet brought in tea and crumpets on a silver tray. The president poured the tea with infinite care.

'You still take no sugar?' he asked. 'It is in the files.'

Qhe smiled again and there was another silence as both men politely sipped their tea.

'Everything is in order with your account?' the president of the bank asked. 'There are no problems?'

'None at all,' Qhe answered, 'but you had better look at this.'

He opened his briefcase and withdrew five files. He looked quickly through them, put one aside and replaced the other four. Then he opened the file and took out three pieces of typed notepaper, each carefully but flamboyantly signed. He handed the first sheet over to the president who took a pair of half-moon spectacles from his breast pocket and studied it. His face remained totally impassive as he read it.

'You will excuse me?' he asked to which Qhe nodded.

The man stood and pressed a button on his desk. Within two seconds, a second dark-suited man had appeared at the door. They whispered together for a few moments then the second man left the room.

'This will only take a minute,' the president of the bank apologized to Qhe. 'More tea?'

Qhe shook his head and waited as the man reappeared with a new piece of paper which they compared with the first.

'Very good,' the president said and his assistant made a discreet exit. He turned to Qhe: 'The code is correct and the signature also.'

'Of course.' Qhe nodded.

The president now looked expectantly up at Qhe. He had always been impressed by the calm behaviour of the monarch of Pashman and had also always ignored the strange rumours that surrounded him. His Majesty was a perfect client and that was what mattered. Qhe handed over the other two sheets of paper.

The president readjusted his half-moon spectacles and began reading. He started by reading casually, but after the first paragraph the muscles around his neck and chin began to tighten. At the second paragraph, his face began to whiten and he could hardly bring himself to read on. His hands now shaking slightly he walked to his desk and poured himself a tumbler of water. The glass trembled as he raised it to his lips. He swallowed, carefully replaced the tumbler and read the second page.

There was nothing that he could do. The instructions were totally explicit and completely legal. But never, never ever in his life . . . He coughed to clear his throat.

'Is there anything that might make you reconsider?' he asked.

'No,' Qhe smiled. 'Nothing.'

'And this includes the most recent deposits?'

'Everything. The instructions are clear, aren't they?'

'Perfectly,' the president answered. 'Of course, it will take a short while to execute.'

'It must be done by tomorrow,' Qhe said firmly.

'Tomorrow?'

'Tomorrow,' Qhe reaffirmed. 'That's not impossible, is it?'

The president shook his head. If it had been impossible, his bank would have been breaking every rule in the stringent code book.

'I assure you,' Qhe said comfortingly, 'that yours is not the only bank involved.'

The president gulped at the implications. Never, never

ever in his life . . .

'But,' he said, 'security arrangements will have to be made.'

'That is under control.'

'And the international implications?'

'It is spread,' Qhe answered, 'very evenly through the various currencies. We haven't left anyone out, have we?'

'No, no. It is very correctly distributed.'

'Good.'

Qhe stood to shake the banker's hand, but the man hardly saw him move. He was perplexed and confused. In the whole range of his experience and in the entire history of the banking profession, he could find no reason or justification for this act.

Qhe held out his hand and, hardly knowing what he was doing, the banker took it.

'Why?' he asked. 'Why?'

'It is for the best,' Qhe answered enigmatically.

A few minutes later, he had left the building and was walking through Zurich to the next of his calls.

TWENTY-TWO

At the small abandoned airstrip near Toulon, Qhe and fifteen of his men knelt in silent prayer. They had formed a small circle and were bringing down a stream of white energy which they passed between themselves and then concentrated into Qhe. He would need every molecule of power for what was to come. His trust was in God. His trust was in the divine thrust of evolution. But in the battle that was to come, his trust had to be in himself.

Even when the distant sound of the approaching jet could be heard, they continued praying, but each man felt his stomach quiver with a tense anticipation. Only when the noise had become deafening did they finally stand and move back.

The private aircraft skidded on the runway, throwing up a huge trail of yellow dust, and came to a halt. Qhe and his men walked towards it, and when the fuselage door opened, they fell to their knees resting their heads on the ground. First to emerge from the plane were twenty of the Prophet's young boys. As usual, they were naked and they pranced down the steps and began dancing and skipping on the runway. They laughed and giggled, overwhelmingly excited by the travelling.

Next came two dozen attendants who, as before, were dressed in their long purple robes with purple gauze scarves hiding their faces. Then *he* came forth.

Standing in the brilliant sunshine, framed by the glittering metal of the plane's fuselage, he looked more magnificent than ever. His body gleamed with power and strength. The grey silver curls of his hair and beard shone as if sculpted by the greatest silversmith. His eyes were huge and glowing, and his smile of intense satisfaction was a delight to behold. His mind and his true self, however, were a festering cesspool of disgusting evil. When today was over the world would be his. He would be the most powerful man on earth. The wealthiest, the most adored, supreme, reigning over everything. His years, centuries, of planning would come to fruition – and he would rule forever.

He looked down at Qhe's humble figure and roared with laughter.

'My little monarch, my little king!' he shouted. 'Raise yourself from the ground! Embrace your benefactor for he loves you! You have served him perfectly!'

Qhe shyly looked up from the ground and his eyes moist with emotional tears he looked up at the Prophet.

'All glory to you,' Qhe moaned.

'Glory, glory,' his warriors echoed, their eyes still fixed on the earth.

'The world adores you. The world awaits you,' Qhe intoned.

'Come. Rise. Come to my arms,' the Prophet shouted.

Qhe slowly raised himself from the ground and then ran to the man like one of the children. He allowed himself to be hugged in the Prophet's gargantuan embrace.

'It goes well,' the Prophet whispered. 'I can feel it within me. How many await me?'

'The whole world. The whole world,' Qhe answered quickly and enthusiastically. 'Oh master, it is all too wonderful. The energies are perfect. The forces in absolute harmony. I even feel that the stars themselves are singing a special hymn to your coming. No one has ever seen or felt anything like it. Your aura expands to fill the whole planet. You *are* the planet. You *are* everything. you make the sun rise in the east, set in the west. You fill –'

'Quiet, my child, quiet!' the Prophet ordered. 'There will be time enough for this when today is over. For the moment let us be silent. Let us savour it all in stillness. Let us savour my glory.'

He roared with laughter again and within his monstrous booming laugh Qhe heard the vicious cackle of a sinister old man of demonic powers. Laugh, old man, laugh, Qhe thought, shortly you shall wither into tears.

He knelt to kiss the Prophet's feet and then stood and

took his hand. He then led the party across the airstrip to a small squadron of helicopters which was piloted by his men.

'He shall come down out of the skies!' the Prophet boomed. 'How true! How very true!'

In perfect formation, the helicopters took off and made a course eastwards along the French Mediterranean coast. As they reached Saint Tropez, they could see that the six-lane motorway beneath had a bumper to bumper traffic jam that disappeared into the distance.

'For you, master. For you,' Qhe said, his voice trembling with adoration.

For a second the Prophet's eyes became misty. Oh it was true, really true. No longer did he have to remain unrecognized and unknown.

'How they need me,' he sighed. 'How the little termites need me.'

'You have seen nothing yet,' Qhe said laughing gleefully. 'It is beyond my wildest dreams.'

'But not beyond mine,' the Prophet answered. 'As the years pass I will teach you my vision. You will fully understand.'

Qhe nodded happily and kissed the Prophet's hand. They passed over Frejus and Saint Raphael and now, not only was there the interminable traffic jam but also thousands, hundreds of thousands, of walking people.

'They will be too late for you,' Qhe said.

'But they *will* feel my presence,' the Prophet answered cunningly.

Then, as they approached the Cape of Antibes, the Prophet sighed with true and infinite satisfaction. Looking inland to the hills behind Antibes and Juan les Pins, the countyside was covered with innumerable people fanning out from one central point in the hills. This point was a three mile wide natural amphitheatre and sitting within its confines were over a million, perhaps even two million, people. At the apex of the amphitheatre, there was a natural rise that made a platform and upon this had been constructed a huge stage. On either side of this stage for fifty yards was a fifty foot high bank of loudspeakers.

'You have done brilliantly,' the Prophet applauded his apprentice. 'I shall play with those people, those slugs, like the moon moving the tides of the sea! Their waves of adoration shall give me power beyond your comprehension! With my invisible cohorts, all shall be mine.'

'Ah,' Qhe whispered, 'you have brought your spirits.'

'They are all around, my unseen servants,' came the smiling answer. 'Together we shall mould the energies.'

Qhe nodded joyfully, but inwardly shuddered.

'And where shall we spend the night?' the Prophet suddenly asked. 'Buckingham Palace or Versailles? The Kremlin or the White House? For as certain as the sun will rise tomorrow, tonight humanity will be a pebble in my hands.'

'There couldn't be a better time,' Don Gillamo said, wringing his hands and looking up at the passing helicopters from the poolside of the Eden Roc Hotel.

Goldino nodded and smiled.

'Altogether,' Gillamo continued, 'this day is going to knock the world for six.'

He drained his glass of scotch and both men walked slowly back into the hotel and made their way to the telex room. An American businessman in bermuda shorts was using it and Goldino clicked his fingers. Immediately three of his bodyguards appeared. Two of them walked forward and took the unsuspecting man by each arm. They then just lifted him up and carried him out. At the door he gathered himself sufficiently to protest and, in return, received a sharp blow to his groin. He collapsed groaning and was removed.

Goldino had taken no notice of this, but went directly to the telex machine. He took a small black book from his jacket which contained the addresses of the five banks and the secret codes for the accounts.

His hands moving like a piano virtuoso's, he punched out his five messages. He then whistled and wiped the sweat from his forehead. He looked to Gillamo who smiled back nervously.

'That's it then,' he said gulping.

'Just the confirmation,' Goldino agreed.

'Boy, this is the heaviest, isn't it?'

'The very heaviest.'

Both men's faces were tired and drawn. They had been unable to sleep for several nights in anticipation of all this. They knew that nothing could go wrong. Every cog was in place. Every gear greased. It was foolproof. It was set up perfectly. God, it was even legal! But it was big, so big.

'This will make the family the most powerful syndicate on earth,' said Gillamo bubbling over with excitement.

'I know. Just shut up. I'm not a child.'

Goldino drummed his fingers along the edge of the machine, making damp sweat-stained finger-prints on the grey metal.

'And you can shut that up as well,' Gillamo hissed. 'You twitch worse than a rattlesnake.'

Goldino stopped moving his fingers and immediately started twitching his foot.

'Come on, come on,' he urged the machine.

Then the first reply began to be typed through. It was short and Goldino ripped the paper out of the machine and looked at it. His eyes screwed up and his mouth went dry.

'What the hell's the matter?' Gillamo asked urgently.

'Shut up and pass me the black book,' came the fast reply. 'I don't know the code. I don't understand what it says.'

Gillamo handed over the book and Goldino feverishly thumbed through it. He found the correct page. His whole body shivered as if struck by lightning and he turned as white as a sheet. He had no chance to say anything before the second reply began to come through. His eyes bulging open, he looked disbelievingly at it.

'What is it?' Gillamo screamed. 'For chrissake what is it?'

The third, fourth and fifth messages came through. They were all the same.

'It – it – it,' Goldino stuttered and put his arm out for support to prevent himself from fainting, 'it says: *account closed.*'

'Closed?'

'Closed!' Goldino shrieked.

'Phone them! Don't trust a lousy machine! Phone them!'

As if in a dream, Goldino nodded and his hand reached out for the telephone.

'There is no need for that,' a voice said. 'What you have read is true.'

Gillamo and Goldino spun round to see the smiling faces of five Pashmani warriors.

'Qhe just wanted a description of your expressions when you found out,' one of them said.

'All of it?' Gillamo asked dreamily. 'All the family's money as well? All of it?'

The Pashmanis nodded. Gillamo let out a cry like a wounded bear and hurled himself at the men who neatly side-stepped and locked his arms from behind.

'He would also like you both to watch the finale,' the warrior said. 'He thinks you will find it instructive.'

The two dazed Dons were led away. Their minds could not grasp what had happened. It was insanity, a nightmare, none of it real. Everything was lost. The family would kill them for this. The family – what would the family be without its money? A hundred years of work and saving disappeared. No, they did not even want to try to cope with the idea.

Their sensation of fantasy was heightened by the helicopter waiting on the beach to lift them up and away towards the hills. Five miles away from the natural amphitheatre, they began to hear an insistent droning noise that broke through even the sound of the helicopter's engines. Goldino's and Gillamo's look of bewilderment deepened.

'What the hell is that?' Gillamo asked.

'The people,' the warrior answered, 'All those people down there.'

For the first time, the two Dons realized that they were flying over a huge sea of human bodies. It was an awesome sight heightened by the strange sound made by the crowd.

Millions of leaflets had been distributed instructing the
eople that, having seen a squadron of helicopters passing
verhead, they should all commence to sound out the holy
ame of *om*. When the helicopters had flown over, two
illion faces had turned towards the sky. *He! He* was
ming, two million minds had thought and, a few seconds
ter, two million voices had begun to chant out *om*. Imme-
iately the crowd had formed into one great unity held
gether by the insistent vibrations of the holy hindu sound.

The Prophet now waited, surrounded only by the twenty
aked boys, on the other side of the rising hill behind the
age. He stood tall and dignified, tuning himself into the
ll of the throng. Around him, invisible in the air, hovered
e army of spirits, demons and devils that served him so
ell in the desert. Also invisible was the thread of energy
at linked him to the great astral cube in the desert, the
ndensed mass of energy which he had so carefully built
nd increased over the centuries. The Prophet was pre-
aring himself to grasp the very souls of everyone in the
owd and he was almost ready.

Also preparing himself was Qhe. In the two hundred
ard deep fenced-off area between the stage and the crowd,
he knelt directly facing the platform. Immediately behind
im was Willard and behind Willard, fanning out in the
ape of a 'V', were the Pashmani warriors. These men
ere acting like a psychic magnifying-glass in the sun,
cking in the psychic rays of the two million strong crowd
nd focusing them into Willard and Qhe.

All of them were tuned into the fanaticism, aspiration
nd devotion of the people. The energies were a strange and
owerful mixture. Every person in the crowd had come
ere with an intense personal desire to see the truth and be
art of some stupendous religious experience. For them the
rophet would provide the answers to everything. Even
ose cynical observers subconsciously desired to be part of
great and wondrous happening.

But what had led all these people to so intensely want
nd need this imminent revelation? Their lives lacked
eace and joy. They all felt that the planet earth and

humanity was not treating them reasonably. It was an unjust and unfair life. They had financial troubles, emotional troubles, mental troubles. All these they wanted solved – and each man and woman there projected the solution onto the Prophet. These people were naïve. Their energies were neither good nor evil, but the Prophet planned to draw into himself their negative desires, their selfish wishes, their greedy hopes.

Qhe led Willard and the Pashmani warriors in their occult meditation. First they had completely calmed their bodies and emptied their minds. Then they had let themsleves become one with the vibrations of the crowd, receptively tuning into the mass desire-form and thought-form. When they had felt themselves to be in true esoteric sympathy with the mass feeling, they had begun to draw the energy into themselves.

To a clairvoyant observer, it looked as if a great mist and cloud of emotional and mental matter enveloping and hovering over the people was being drawn forward to Qhe and his men, where it passed through them and then swirled up into the air like a monstrous tornado-like vortex

Qhe and Willard now began their most tortuous psychic work. It needed a delicacy and mental precision of incredible finesse. Above all it needed perfectly balanced concentration which was almost impossible in the situation. Their minds were literally being rocked and buffeted by the power and anticipation of the crowd. The echoing drone of the *om* made their eardrums vibrate and quiver, and their bodies tingled with a strange electricity.

The two men telepathically probed into the vortex of energies above them searching for that fundamental thread of good and positive power that existed in every man. If a man wanted peace for himself, he wanted peace for everyone, for without it, he himself would never have that peace. If he wanted food, everyone should have it. If he wanted joy, the whole world should thrill with happiness. Qhe and Willard strained every mental atom to grasp hold of this golden matter.

Suddenly the whole crowd fell silent. There was a deep

and eery hush, broken only by the occasional groan and moan from men and women for whom it was too much. At the rise of the hill behind the stage, a silver golden glow like an enormous halo was beginning to appear to rise into the air.

TWENTY-THREE

He, the Prophet, appeared like a flaming god over the hill and he looked unbelievably magnificent. As one, the multitude gasped and lowered their heads.

Surrounded by a circle of shimmering phosphorescent energy, he leviated to float some thirty feet in the air. Dressed in a robe of glowing woven gold thread, he beamed his wondrous smile and opened wide his arms in blessing. Again, the multitude gasped and moaned.

For five minutes, he did nothing but float there and allow the crowd to thrill at his wondrous appearance. His mind reached out and immediately felt the selfish and greedy needs and desires of the people before him. Oh glorious moment! he thought. He sucked in these energies like a parched tree in the desert sucking in water. He then projected them into the spirits that hovered around him and fed them down the psychic thread to his astral cube in the Sahara.

He came forward fifty feet and the crowd reacted with an overwhelming surge towards him. He took this energy too, and sent it to the cube where it gained even greater force which he then pulled back to himself.

Once more he came forward and a mood of blissful and frantic hysteria now permeated the people. It was *he*. Truly, the Prophet of all ages had come again! All the promises had been fulfilled! They saw *him*! *He* was with them!

In those moments of great tension, men and women began to weep. They hugged each other. They blessed each other. They were one body – one body together to worship the Prophet.

He now moved over the stage and then gently lowered himself to stand a few yards behind the microphones.

'Bless you!' he roared. 'Bless you!'

'Bless you as well,' Qhe whispered.

A great wave of uncontrollable devotion passed through he crowd towards him, towards *their* Prophet.

'Bless you! I bless you!' he repeated, his voice echoing ut, a hundred thousand times amplified by the massive anks of loudspeakers.

Unseen by the Prophet, Qhe now raised his hand and mmediately his warriors also began to chant: *bless you, less you.* They sang it gently but insistently and, within a ninute, the section of the crowd nearest them also took up he chant. Gradually, it was being picked up by everyone and hortly the whole mass was singing out *bless you, bless you.*

The Prophet's smile widened and again he opened his rms to receive the people's energies. His eyes blazed with lory for even he had not expected such a beautifully con-erted expression of devotion. He wallowed in it like a child olling in mud. I have them, he whispered to himself. I have hem like no one has ever had them before. The children, he pathetic mindless children. Do they know what they ive me? Do they have the slightest notion of it all? I have hem. I have the people. I have the planet. At last mine, nly mine.

He closed his eyes for a moment to absorb fully the plendour of it all. Pathetic people! Pathetic crippled vorms! Their vision of glory is nought but my power! My ower! The slugs, the human slugs! I crush them beneath ny feet! Even that is too good and glorious for them – to be ouched by me! Do I feel any remorse? None! Not the lightest hint of regret or guilt? None! Would I not prefer to vork within the divine plan? The divine plan is mine – nine alone!

The Prophet's eyes opened. His smile had suddenly dis-ppeared. His face was tense and furious. Never had such uestions entered his mind. Never! His eyes narrowed. His mile returned and he looked around. The crowd was still inging their chant, but it was no longer as comforting and narvellous to him.

'Bless you!' he himself roared, hurling his own sinister nergy out at them.

He waited a second for a wave of negative power to

return to him, but there was none. Immediately, he drew down energy from his spirits and from the desert and willed it to thread through the crowd. Once more he felt the quality of energy that he desired from them and he inwardly sneered at them for being so naïve as to have the slghtest good atom of energy for him. But then again, he felt their mood changing. He drew yet more energy from his spirits and reservoir, and then something instinctively made him look down.

His eyes were met by Qhe's. In that second, the Prophet knew that he had been betrayed. His mouth twisted into a crooked and cunning grin. He reorientated his forces and threw the full might of his power at Qhe.

Qhe shuddered slightly, but continued staring deep into the Prophet. He had locked himself into that vortex of good and divine energy and, like a dam slowly opening its floodgates, was letting it pour through him and onto the Prophet. He, as Qhe, did not exist. He was purely a channel for the flood of force that he was willing through himself while Willard and the warriors worked to intensify and keep the flow coming.

The crowd could see nothing except for an enigmatic change of expression on their Prophet's face and they took this to mean that he was deeply moved by their attitude of devotion. With greater fervour than ever they sang out their chant of blessing to him. But the prophet now was neither hearing nor seeing the crowd. His whole being was focused on Qhe, on this worm who was daring to usurp him. Silently he sounded his demonic invocations and ordered the spirits to attack the man. They swooped down to warp, confuse and destroy Qhe's brain, but they could not approach within fifty feet of thim so great was the power of light around him.

Kill him, kill him, the Prophet mentally commanded. The spirits dove downwards once more, but they could no more touch Qhe than a man can walk through a brick wall. The Prophet sounded out yet another great magical conjuration and even greater, more powerful evil spirits came to serve him. *Kill,* he commanded again. *Serve me and kill.*

Qhe felt the new malevolent presences and willed that the energy passing through him should strike them like thunderbolts. Astrally, each spirit and demon screamed in hellish agony at the touch of the golden force.

The Prophet raised his hands and charged that all the power that he had ever known should strike down this interfering pest. A grey stream of energy that even the crowd could see shot from his hands and was caught in the silver web around Qhe and then sent spinning upwards into the tornado of light. But with this surge of power, the Prophet had for a moment counterbalanced all that Qhe was willing at him. The energies were locked and balanced. Everything was suddenly cemented into a psychic stalemate.

Both Qhe and the Prophet felt this sudden impasse, and now not for one split second did they dare take their eyes off each other. With all the energies locked in balance, it was a matter of personal power. If one of them looked away, he would immediately be overpowered. All this pleased the Prophet for he had watched Qhe in the days before and he knew that this snivelling creature who had begged to be his lieutenant had not a hundredth of the necessary power. He remembered Qhe crouched on the ground kissing his feet. The Prophet smiled and willed Qhe to surrender.

Qhe's face remained impassive. He, too, remembered the humiliations of the previous days, but he wiped them from his mind. He would win this war with the force of his soul and not with the force of his personality. No personality, no matter how great and monstrous, could defeat the energies of a soul.

As the Prophet geared himself up into an intense and furious venom against this man, so Qhe opened up himself to let the dynamism of his soul power descend. The two men's eyes were watering and their face muscles tense and aching. The Prophet imagined Qhe to be no larger than an ant and willed him to break down and be crushed. And Qhe begged that love and light should pour through him onto this unfortunate and evil being. He looked for the pathetic old man who hid inside the mammoth body of the

Prophet. He looked for the pathetic withered old man, for to this creature he could give his sympathy.

The Prophet felt Qhe seeking this vision and puffed up his chest and rippled his muscles. *No use*, Qhe telepathed, *I have seen you once and I shall see you again. I see you again. I see you now.*

Never! the Prophet mentally screamed back. *I am he, the most glorious man of power.*

Pathetic old man. Senile hermit of hopeless dreams and visions. You have my sympathy. I love you.

Love is charcoal ash to me. Nothing! Come, worm, desist. You have a few seconds longer – no more!

Old man, old man. Even your fleshy robes are transparent. I see you. Your hopes are those of a demented and pathetic mind. Come back into the light. You are not yet totally lost.

Die in darkness! Be enveloped in black! Tortured for ever! You live a lie! My power drowns you!

Your power is nothing. It is like a morning mist, disappearing in the sun of my love. Be loved! Be lighted!

The Prophet's mind spun and shook as he saw Qhe's face melt to appear like the rising golden orb of the sun. He closed his eyes and saw a thousand, a million sparkling stars. These stars were singing in glorious harmony, making the fantastic music of the cosmos.

No! His mind screamed like a man falling from the highest tower. No!

He opened his eyes and Qhe was now walking towards him. It cannot be! It cannot be! he silently screamed a thousand times. And now he could hear again the chanting of the crowd:

'Bless you. Bless you. Bless you.'

His hands wanted to move to cover his ears from this offending noise. He needed no blessing. He desired no blessing. These people were worms – worms for him to command. But his hands would not move up to his head. He saw Qhe stepping onto the stage and he wished to rush and crush this man with his bare hands. His feet, too, would not move. He was held rigid and immobile.

He could feel his personal power slipping away like a sponge being squeezed dry. He silently vibrated out his demonic calls and conjurations, but he no longer had the force to reach them. Looking up, Qhe's eyes were all that he could see and they were irresistibly seducing him, irresistibly holding them. He could no longer fight. Every ounce of strength that had been his was gone.

Smile at the people, Qhe telepathed. The Prophet smiled. *Now raise your hands to bless them*. He raised them and the crowd roared their chant of blessing. *Now whisper gently that they should be silent*.

'Please,' the Prophet's voice came over the loud-speakers. 'Please some silence.'

Within a second, the crowd was silent. *He*, yes, *he* was about to speak!

Repeat after me word by word, Qhe telepathed, *and always smile. I have come . . .*

'I have come . . .' the Prophet spoke '. . . to teach . . . My time is short . . . I come only in the name of He who has sent me . . . Always there is love . . . Always there is light . . . Think on this ever . . . know it ever . . . It is truth . . . Love . . . Light . . His power . . . He wishes world peace. He wishes world harmony. He blesses the men of goodwill everywhere who work to this. The barriers must be destroyed. The barriers of race, of money, of politics, of religion must all come down . . . I come to sacrifice in his name.'

As he spoke, three giant transport helicopters had appeared in the sky behind. Hanging from each one was a huge net carrying a cargo. The three helicopters flew until they were directly overhead the area in front of the stage and they then released their nets. There was a momentous thudding noise as the thousands and thousands of bundles hit the earth. The people at the front of the crowd could see what they were, but they did not believe it. There were millions, billions of banknotes. Bundle after bundle of money. Pounds, dollars, francs, marks – every conceivable currency.

One of the warriors now passed Qhe a lighted torch

which he, in turn, passed over to the Prophet. *Hold it high. Speak with a sense of glory,* Qhe told him. *Ever in the past . . .*

'Ever in the past . . .' the Prophet continued speaking, his voice mellow and golden, '. . . has man sacrificed that which is most dear to him. Through it, he has learned the unimportance of these things and has then known about truth and reality. Let the material world of money have no importance for man.'

At these words, the people at the front of the crowd believed what they had seen. *Money,* they whispered, *more money than in the world.* For a minute, the Prophet's words were drowned by the drone of the crowd as everyone was told what the helicopters had brought.

'Let it have no intense meaning for man,' the Prophet continued. 'Let all men and women see it in clear perspective.'

He raised the torch high above his head.

'Let the greed,' he said firmly, 'of men – of nations – of all peoples – be gone.'

Then, erect and dignified, he walked down the stage and to the ground and stood beside the mountain of banknotes. He placed the torch to the paper.

Though under the control of Qhe, the Prophet's mind was still working and he knew in full consciousness all that he had just done. No words could approach a true description of his tortured and mangled emotions. He was destroying all that he had built and he had done it with a smile and giving God's blessing. For hundreds of years every thought of his, every emotion, every feeling had been solely orientated to gaining power for evil. In barely sixty minutes he had wiped it all out.

He looked into the fire and in the roaring flames he had a clairvoyant vision of his evil maze of caverns in the Sahara and of the glistening black cube surrounded by the huge astral form. Also, he saw spirits dancing and shrieking with laughter, pointing at him, taunting and jeering. As his mind reached out to grasp the full truth of his total failure, he saw in the fire the form of the black cube begin to tarnish and crack. The grey astral cloud was evaporating as the tornado of light that had overshadowed Qhe entered to fully neutralise and balance its negative energy.

Wincing, tears in his eyes, the Prophet watched all this, watched as it all caved in upon itself, as the cube disintegrated into dust, as the caverns collapsed, as the desert reclaimed all that was its own. And then he saw a vision of himself. He saw his herculean body shrinking and thinning. The silken curls of his hair straightening, then falling from his head. His skin tightening and wrinkling. His eyes narrowing. His lips thinning.

'Oh God!' he cried in abject terror. 'Save me! Save me!'

The hollow echoing sound of the old man's voice that was his own threw him into a new reality. Panic burning in his eyes, he looked desperately to Qhe who watched calmly and impassively. The old man could not bear to be seen like that. It was the final horrifying twist. Of all things, this he could not allow and this he could stop.

He smiled cunningly and then, with a terrifying rattling scream, he threw himself into the flames. His second scream piercingly broke through the air as he felt the fire burning and eating at his flesh.

The crowd saw and heard nothing. When the fire had burned down, they knew only this: Their Prophet had come – and now he was gone. And he had taught a lesson.

Two weeks later, Qhe, Willard and Marie de Baldeau were sitting on the edge of the lake beside Qhe's palace in Pashman. Their trousers were rolled up and their feet dangled in the water beside the lilies.

Beside them was a small transistor radio tuned into the BBC World Service. Willard was feeding grain to the tame swans and geese. Marie was taking photographs. And Qhe was humming happily to himself as he carefully inserted the Palermo diamond into the eye of the ivory bull, the present for his baby son. Gillamo had been happy to sell the diamond to him for any price.

All three stopped what they were doing for a few seconds as they listened to news of the success of the International

Monetary Conference. Having heard it, they smiled and then Willard switched off the radio. Qhe put a finishing touch to the position of the diamond eye in the bull.

'There,' Qhe said. 'It is done.'

'It's beautiful,' Marie said.

'Yes, very beautiful,' Willard agreed.

Qhe stroked his hand along the ivory, the inlaid gold and the hundreds of sparkling gems.

'May I photograph it?' Marie asked.

'In a second,' Qhe answered.

He leaned forward and lowered the priceless bull into the water until it was completely submerged. Without the slightest change of expression on his face, he removed his hands and the bull was no longer in them. He had let it sink to the bottom of the lake.

'No,' Marie gasped. 'You couldn't have.'

'Oh yes he has,' Willard chuckled. 'What better way of protecting his child?'

The three of them remained sitting there until nightfall while on the other side of the lake the Pashmani people smiled and nodded at the sight of their happy king.